AN ACCIDENT OF LOVE . . .

"I trust you are not hurt, sir?" Karenza said gently as the tall man finally regained his balance and moved towards her.

"And what do you mean by letting that misbegotten cur attack my horse!" His voice showed a sad lack of respect for the presence of a lady, and there was little doubt that he was extremely angry.

Karenza eyed him speculatively, aware that his anger was due more to injured dignity than physical pain. Still, he should not address her in such a rude manner.

"I must apologise if my dog upset you, but although he may have startled your horse, it was not really his fault that you fell off!"

There was a stunned silence, then his lordship gave a short bark of laughter as he came closer to her. Karenza regarded him with a candid stare; he was a most striking-looking man, quite unlike anyone in her immediate circle.

A cool smile curled his lips. "Fair maiden, you have rendered me horseless and as much bruised in my feelings as in my body. You therefore owe me recompense. Come, give me a kiss for my pains!"

The Reluctant Heir

Shirley Callander

DIAMOND BOOKS, NEW YORK

THE RELUCTANT HEIR

A Diamond Book / published by arrangement with the author

PRINTING HISTORY
Diamond edition / June 1992

ISBN: 1-55773-724-X

The Reluctant Heir

 1

"Am I to understand that along with the title and the estate I've also inherited responsibility for a pack of females!" The new Viscount Darnborough allowed a hint of incredulity to tinge his voice.

"In a manner of speaking, my lord." Mr Ponsonby gave an apologetic little cough.

"How many are there?"

"Five, my lord."

"Five! Good God!"

A wintry smile crossed the lawyer's features as he busied himself with sorting through the pile of documents in front of him, while his noble client absorbed the highly unwelcome news he had just imparted. A slight frown transfixed his lordship's dark face as he absently drummed long, well-formed fingers on the arms of his chair.

The viscount was a striking-looking man, with a rather swarthy countenance and curiously light grey eyes which glinted from beneath straight, dark brows. The aquiline nose and firm chin gave added strength to an already imposing visage. Of above-average height, his powerfully built shoulders and athletically muscular thighs and legs were the envy of many a would-be beau. It was difficult to judge his age, but he was, in fact, in his early thirties. Dressed informally in breeches and top boots, he wore his clothes with an air of careless elegance. His boots were highly polished, his neckcloth arranged to a nicety and his coat, cut by Weston, fit him perfectly.

The silence was abruptly broken by Lord Darnborough. "Was my relative quite sane when he made this will?" he demanded acidly.

"Certainly, my lord!" Mr Ponsonby sounded scandalised that such a slur should be cast on his late client's character, though honesty forced him secretly to admit there had been times when he had asked himself that same question. He pursed his lips before continuing. "You were not acquainted, sir, with your late cousin?" he probed delicately, allowing a little of his surprise to enter his voice.

Lord Darnborough raised his eyes from his frowning contemplation of the document in front of him and looked directly at the lined face of the older man. "I am sure that you have a greater awareness of the facts relating to the quarrel which led to the breach between my grandfather and his uncle than I have," he said dryly. "As for myself, the connection was a very remote one, and I know nothing of that side of the family, except for what I have learned from you today. I cannot comprehend why my cousin, if I may call him that, should entrust his daughters to my care. Nor do I understand," he added in a more forbidding tone, "why he should imagine that I would be prepared to share Darnborough Hall with them. You must arrange for them to move to the Dower House."

An almost amused gleam entered the lawyer's shrewd eyes. "I'm afraid that will not be possible, my lord. Perhaps I should explain the situation more fully," he added hastily, as his lordship regarded him with a look of haughty displeasure. "When the fifth viscount made his will, towards the end of his final illness, he was unaware of the sad death of your elder brother, Sir Horace. It was only by chance that he remembered reading in the *Gazette* some six years ago of Sir Henry's marriage, and it was this knowledge which encouraged the late Lord Darnborough to entrust his daughters to the care of Sir Horace and his heirs. He felt that Lady Wentworth would provide them with the mother they lacked."

The new viscount allowed himself a brief thought of what his giddy young sister-in-law's reaction would have been had this event occurred. Married to a man twenty years her senior, she would scarcely have enjoyed playing the role of mama to five young ladies. Happily, she had been spared this ordeal, and since her remarriage to Sir Reginald Mainwaring had passed beyond the Wentworth family orbit.

"It was to be regretted, my lord," Mr Ponsonby continued, "that due to your absence abroad for the past six months I was unable to acquaint you with the details concerning your inheritance at an earlier date. Indeed, it was most unfortunate that you were not able to attend the late viscount's funeral." There was a reproachful note to the lawyer's words.

"Don't talk flummery to me, Ponsonby! It is unlikely that I should feel any great concern over missing the funeral of a man I never knew, let alone regret being unaware of the fact that I was his heir. I cannot say that I am even pleased at what Society would no doubt term my good fortune. I have no need of a title or what appears to be an impoverished estate, and certainly not the guardianship of five females!" There was no mistaking the viscount's abhorrence of the burden being thrust upon him.

Mr Ponsonby offered no comment to these embittered words. Indeed, he would have been hard put to have found one, for he was well aware that the new heir had already succeeded not only to the baronetcy left vacant by the death of his elder brother, but also to the large estate which accompanied it. Even by the most conservative estimate, the viscount was reckoned to be worth every penny of thirty thousand pounds a year, a fortune guaranteed to make him the irresistible target of every match-making mama with an eligible daughter to hand. He had been courted, hunted and fawned over so often by beauties desiring to make such an advantageous match that it was not surprising he should have developed a contempt for them and treated their advances with cynical disdain, realising it was his wealth and position they really coveted. What his feelings would be on learning the remaining terms of the will, Mr Ponsonby shuddered to think.

As if reading his thoughts, the light grey eyes held a speculative stare as they once more fastened on the lawyer. "I believe you said it would not be possible for the young ladies to move into the Dower House. You must forgive me for being a trifle dull-witted today, but perhaps you could explain why this should be the case."

Mr Ponsonby gazed at the viscount reflectively. Had it not been possible that his patron might consider it an impertinence, he would have allowed himself a little chuckle at his lordship's expense. Instead, he cleared his throat and, straightening his shoulders, selected his words with care.

"You will not, my lord, be aware of the fact that when your great-great-grandfather rebuilt Darnborough Hall after the fire of 1716, he erected it on the boundary of the entailed part of the estate. Later additions to the house in 1749 and 1790 were built on the unentailed land and were thus not automatically inherited by the heir to the main estate. It is the additional west wing which has been left, without any restrictions, to Miss Karenza and her sisters for so long as any one of them has need of a home."

Carefully avoiding the stunned gaze of his noble client, the lawyer continued to speak. "Of course, their income is quite modest, since the tenanted farms and village lie within the entailed estate and form part of your inheritance. It is with regret that I have to inform you those returns are not as great as they could be." The lawyer hesitated a moment before adding, "Unfortunately the late viscount was much interested in the turf, and a large part of his income went on more pleasurable pursuits than improving his lands."

The viscount's black eyebrows snapped together in a frown. He rose to his feet and moved over to the handsome-looking Adams fireplace before turning, to regard his legal adviser once more. "This is damnable! Is there no way that I can avoid this inheritance and its infamous obligations?"

"None, my lord." Mr Ponsonby did not add that he had already thoroughly investigated every possibility of having the will declared invalid. Nor did he explain that he had done so at the urgent request of the late viscount's eldest daughter, who with a sad lack of filial respect declared that, ill or not, her father must have been badly foxed at the time of making it to have placed his children in such an invidious position. To which she had added that surely dear Mr Ponsonby would be able to find a way out of their dreadful predicament. To have a total stranger—the very one who was to take their old home from them—as their lawful guardian was not to be tolerated! Alas, it had not been possible, for none other than Nathaniel Meaker, Mr Ponsonby's legal partner, had been responsible for drawing up the offending document, and he was not a man who made mistakes or left legal loopholes to benefit those who might wish to challenge his expertise.

Lord Darnborough, absentmindedly swinging his quizzing glass, cast a further, somewhat unfathomable stare at the elderly lawyer before saying in a more resigned tone of voice, "I must confess to feeling a trifle uneasy over the fact that none of these young ladies is married or even betrothed. Is there perhaps some dark secret concerning them which you have not yet revealed to me?" In spite of his almost bantering tone, the viscount's expression showed little humour.

Mr Ponsonby shot his client an indignant glance before answering rather frostily, "The Misses Coningsby are most delightful young ladies for whom I have the very highest regard."

"You profoundly relieve me, my dear fellow. But, pray, explain why such paragons of virtue remain unwed." There was a note of cold disbelief in the viscount's voice which irritated the older man and caused him to answer with more passion than was his wont.

"Miss Karenza and Miss Sapphira, who recently attained their twentieth birthday, are considered to be extremely attractive and charming young ladies and could no doubt be wed had they so wished."

"Both twenty!"

"Twins, my lord. Followed by Miss Cressidia, who is nearly nineteen; then Miss Drusilla, just sixteen; and finally, the youngest of the family, Miss Arabella, who is but fourteen years of age." He paused before adding smoothly, "Your lordship will be able to judge their attributes for yourself when you meet your charges, an event which I trust will occur in the very near future, as you will no doubt wish to rearrange the residence to enable you to meet your obligations in the best possible manner. Of course—"

He was interrupted without ceremony. "My good man, are you seriously suggesting that I should personally take on the running of a household of frippery females? You must be out of your senses! What they need is some matron to chaperone them and to supervise their activities, not a bachelor."

"I agree with much of what you say, sir. It came as a great shock to me to learn of your single state, but the will appoints you as guardian of the ladies, and the estate needs the presence of its master," returned the lawyer rather gloomily.

"Be that as it may, I have no intention of making my home at Darnborough Hall," replied his lordship in a very decisive voice.

There was a discouraging silence before Mr Ponsonby spoke again. Although his tone was meek, there was a slightly humorous gleam in his eyes. "Miss Karenza will no doubt be relieved to hear it, my lord."

"Really, Ponsonby, really! Pray, how am I to take that?" The viscount spoke with quelling hauteur, but his mouth twitched and under their lazy lids his eyes held a gleam of laughter. These signs were not lost on his companion, as he considered how best to inform his client that the Misses Coningsby were as much aghast at the terms of the will as was the new viscount.

"Miss Karenza, who is the elder of the twins, sir, is well accustomed to the administration of the household. Throughout her father's last illness, she also conducted the management of the estate—with the assistance, of course, of the bailiff, Mr Morden. Indeed, my lord, during your absence Miss Karenza has continued to conduct the day-to-day running of your inheritance at my request, for I know none who would be more suitable for such a task. It will not be easy for her to see a stranger in her father's place." He paused and gazed rather doubtfully at Lord Darnborough, who had withdrawn an enamel snuffbox from his pocket and was opening it with a practised flick of his thumb. His dark visage, however, preserved its inscrutability, and Mr

Ponsonby went on in a more earnest tone. "Miss Karenza is fully aware of the delicacy of her position and that of her sisters. Indeed, she has already arranged for an elderly cousin of her mother's, a Miss Rachel Brinton, to render them the protection of her company."

"Then the problem is solved, at least until the family put off their black gloves," said Lord Darnborough decisively. "Miss Brinton will remain in residence, whilst I shall confine myself to periodic visits. The elder Miss Coningsby may, if she so wishes, continue to be responsible for the general administration of the household until such a time as I wish to take up my abode there. As for the estate, I will interview Mr Morden and decide what would be the best arrangement for its future. I am sure that my wards will find these plans most acceptable."

"Perhaps, my lord." The lawyer's voice denoted a sense of unease. The viscount looked down at him, his eyebrows slightly raised.

"Unless I am very much mistaken, you have something further to reveal to me, Ponsonby."

Mr Ponsonby, feeling some surprise at his lordship's acumen, sought to communicate his foreboding concerning the ladies Coningsby.

"I do not wish to convey any disrespect for Miss Karenza, sir, but she is a very determined and independent young lady who has no desire to be beholdened to anyone. Since becoming aware of their limited financial circumstances, Miss Karenza, or Miss Coningsby as I should no doubt call her, has required of me to investigate certain ways in which she and her sisters could supplement their income."

Lord Darnborough, correctly interpreting the look of worry on the lawyer's face, smoothly interrupted him. "Which would no doubt concern me. Come, come, don't prevaricate, man. What do they intend to do, sell the family heirlooms?"

Since the viscount's tone held no more than sympathetic interest, Mr Ponsonby was emboldened to speak out.

"Not quite so bad as that, my lord," he replied with a slight smile, which was immediately followed by a deep sigh. "I fear they are considering the use of their part of the house as a seminary for young ladies."

"Oh, my God!" His lordship looked thunderstruck. "I won't have it, Ponsonby. It's bad enough having five females about the place, but a school of them—never!"

"I'm afraid, my lord, that Miss Karenza and Miss Sapphira can do what they wish with their part of the house, if not immediately then as soon as they come of age next year," said the lawyer mournfully. "And they are fully aware of their legal rights."

"They may be aware of their rights, but I'm also fully aware of mine, as well as of my duties as their father's successor. And they do not include allowing my cousins to act in such a manner. They had better not try and cross swords with me on this subject." There was a decidedly grim note to the sixth viscount's voice. He saw that the elderly man was looking still far from satisfied. "Leave it all to me. I promise you that I will protect my charges from themselves!"

"I hope so, my lord. I feel it will not be an easy task, and I have to admit that my sympathies lie, on the whole, with Miss Karenza and her sisters. I pray, sir, that you will try to understand how difficult they find their position when you are with them." There was no mistaking the man's genuine concern.

The viscount smiled. "I shall bear your words in mind, I promise you. I am no ogre and do sincerely sympathize with the sad circumstances in which the ladies find themselves." He turned and pulled the bellrope by the mantel. "Now you shall drink a glass of sherry with me and give me your advice on what the estate requires to put it back in good shape. Then I will consider when it will be most convenient for me to visit Huntingdonshire and meet my young wards."

Not half an hour after the lawyer had departed, having obtained a reluctant commitment from the new heir to visit his inheritance within the sennight, the butler announced a new arrival in satisfied tones.

"Lady Mapping, my lord."

"What the devil brings you to London, Georgie?" His lordship's tone was affable in spite of his words as he went forward to greet his elder sister. Her marriage to a country squire kept her for most of the year in the deep fastness of Hertfordshire, so that her visitations to her brother in London were rare occasions and generally precipitated by some real or imagined domestic crisis.

"My dear Marcus, pray do not fall into such raptures at my appearance. Such a demonstration of affection quite overwhelms me." Her tone was gently satirical as she strolled towards her brother. Grey eyes, so similar to his own, yet much softer, were laughing at him from a comely rather than beautiful face, though its vivacity and kindly humour gave it a rather special attraction of its own.

" 'Tis not your presence, but its very suddenness which fills me with foreboding, my dear," he retorted, lightly kissing her proffered cheek. "Pray, put me out of my suspense, Georgie. What has occasioned the honour of this visit?"

"My very natural desire to learn more of your new inheritance, of course, as well as the need to refurbish my wardrobe. I vow that I'm looking a positive dowd these days."

"How the devil did you learn of the Darnborough legacy? I've only just been acquainted with the facts myself!" the viscount exclaimed.

"If," his sister replied severely, "you had read but one of the numerous letters poor Mr Ponsonby wrote to you, you would have learnt that he has been seeking your whereabouts for the past six months, which, dear brother, included various despairing visits to your beloved sister and other relations in vain attempts to discover the date of your anticipated return to England. I need hardly add that none of us were able to enlighten him!"

Lord Darnborough smiled, but his steady gaze remained on her face. "I must beg your forgiveness in being so discommoding as not to furnish you with my itinerary, but unfortunately my mission on behalf of Lord Castlereagh was a roving one, and I scarce knew one day to the next where I should be, or when."

Well aware that her brother sometimes acted as an unofficial envoy for Britain's skillful Foreign Secretary in the to-ing and fro-ing between Britain and her allies at the end of the long war against her archenemy, Napoleon Bonaparte, there was nothing to surprise her in his explanation. She could not help wishing, however, that his restlessness could find a more comfortable outlet—such as marriage and a family of his own—to occupy him. Absorbed in her own progeny and rarely visiting London, she had only slowly become aware that her younger brother—twelve years separated them—had become a somewhat aloof, cynical man, lacking the friendly warmth which had been so much a part of his nature as a child. It seemed to her that only by falling completely and utterly in love would he perhaps regain the joy in living which he unhappily had lost. The thought of falling in love brought to mind the real purpose of her visit.

"The most vexatious thing has occurred, my dear, on which I require your advice." Lady Mapping raised an anxious face to his. " 'Tis Justin. He has fallen in love and vows that he wishes to marry." Her tones were tragic.

Aware that he was being presented with the main reason for his sister's visit, his lordship gave a long-suffering sigh and sought to alleviate his sister's concern. "I've no doubt he will feel this way several times over the next few years. How old is the brat?"

"Considering you're his uncle, you should certainly know that he is but twenty."

"Then you and Frederick need not concern yourselves—you just forbid the banns," the viscount recommended, showing but scant interest in his nephew's love life.

"I do wish that were all that was necessary," she wailed, "but the matter is more serious than that. He will be of age in four months and states quite categorically that he will marry that scheming hussy!"

Lord Darnborough raised a surprised eyebrow at his sister's unusually strong words, for normally she was a very level-headed woman and not prone to fussing too much over her children. In matters affecting their future, however, she tended to consult her more sophisticated and worldly younger brother in preference to her dearest—yet to be honest, somewhat naive—spouse.

"Who's the girl?" he demanded.

"A lovely-looking hussy whose mother runs a gaming house!"

"What!" exclaimed the viscount incredulously.

"I thought you would appreciate my feelings when I told you." Her ladyship spoke with certain glum satisfaction. "I was never so shocked in all my life as when he told me. I strictly forbade him to tell his dear papa, for I feared my Frederick might suffer a stroke on receiving such news. What can you do to help us, Marcus?"

"For goodness sake, Georgie, the boy's just amusing himself. It don't signify. He'll have changed his mind by next month, I have no doubt."

"I told you, he means to marry her," his sister repeated obstinately.

"Nonsense," his lordship said briskly. "He is not such an idiot as to imagine one marries a woman from a gaming house."

"Then I wish you would tell him so. For he is convinced it is his duty to rescue her from such a life, and no doubt her mother as well. He is completely besotted by the girl. She will utterly ruin him, I know she will!" There was a note of genuine despair in her voice.

The viscount frowned. "You had better tell the young puppy that I wish him to accompany me to Darnborough Hall this coming week. It will give me the opportunity of finding out more about this affair from him."

"He won't come," she answered sadly.

Lord Darnborough gave a short laugh. "Inform young Lochinvar that I wish to acquaint him with his new cousins—five beautiful, defenceless young females, who would no doubt be glad to receive his sympathetic support, certainly after they've met me!" he added grimly.

"What! You're bamming me!" Lady Mapping sat upright, surprise and amusement written across her face.

"Such unbecoming language from a lady, dear sister. You put me to blush."

"Stop trying to prevaricate, Marcus. Do tell me more, for I swear that Mr Ponsonby never so much as mentioned them to me." For a moment she had forgotten her own woes and listened with growing interest to her brother's account of his inheritance.

"Yes, that may be the answer to more than one problem," she murmured somewhat enigmatically as he ended. There was an unusually thoughtful look in her eyes as she regarded her brother's countenance, which still portrayed his distaste of his new responsibilities.

" 'Pon my word, Marcus, I shall ask Justin to visit me here tomorrow, if I may, for he is in town at the moment on a visit to his good friend Felix Laverton. Do permit me to send a footman with a note to him this evening."

"As you wish," said Lord Darnborough languidly. "If you have any problem with the boy, let me know and I will deal with him myself, but I do not feel that he will deny me my request." The degree of certainty in his voice almost caused his sister to protest, but thinking that he was probably right, she desisted.

"Well, I earnestly hope that his sojourn at Darnborough Hall will help to detach him from that awful female"— she paused for a moment before adding, so softly that he failed to catch her words—"and break the ice which now surrounds your own heart, dear brother."

 2

Situated in Huntingdonshire, near the village of Upper Tilling, Darnborough Hall was designated in the guidebooks as being of some interest to the more discerning devotee of English architecture. The original Tudor mansion had been destroyed by fire, an occurrence regarded with some gratitude by its then occupant and his family, who all too frequently had suffered from the cold winds that whistled down long, draughty passages, aided by ill-fitting doors and vast casement windows.

The name of the architect of the new residence was unknown, which was surprising as the building was the work of an accomplished hand. The style of the house was clearly derived from the designs of Sir Christopher Wren, although later generations had enlarged and modified it according to individual whims and tastes. The resulting structure now encompassed a rotunda erected by order of one of the more eccentric viscounts, who had been greatly influenced by a visit to Rome, as well as a more gracious but extremely large west wing in the Palladian style, its magnificent saloon containing a coffered ceiling and a marble fireplace that replicated one in the Ducal Palace in Venice. Dominating the main entrance hall were five great sporting paintings executed about 1730 by John Wootten for the third viscount, who combined a taste for the arts with a

15

passion for sport, a trait inherited with less fortunate results by the fifth Lord Darnborough. The latter, alas, spent more than he could afford in gratifying his love of the equine world, disposing of every available penny of his income either on his racing string or on the slapping great hunters which never numbered fewer than twelve in his stables.

It was, in fact, the need to dispose of the best of these assets that caused the elder Miss Coningsby to seek the advice of the estate bailiff. Together, they now surveyed the few remaining horses, thankful that they were not included as a part of the entailed estate and thus could be still sold for the benefit of the young Misses Coningsby. For as Karenza had stated, with all the frankness of one who has been acquainted with the elderly agent since babyhood, they would need every available penny, especially if Miss Cressidia was to have the benefit of a London Season once they were out of mourning. To which words the old man had nodded his head in vigorous agreement.

They were now standing in front of the stable, which housed the pride of the late viscount's racing string. The great, black stallion within tossed his head restlessly as Karenza sought to stroke the gleaming arched neck with its flowing mane.

"I shall be sorry, Mr Morden, to see Buccaneer leave us. He is truly a most magnificent creature. I shall miss him very much." She gave a deep sigh at the thought of having to part with her favourite mount. "To be sure, he is not an easy animal to ride, but he and I have always got on famously."

"Indeed, ma'am, you have! 'Tis a wicked shame that you should have to be separated from him. Is there no way in which you could retain him for your own use?" Mr Morden's voice was full of kindly understanding, and Karenza flashed him an appreciative smile.

"I fear not. He consumes a prodigious amount and is vastly expensive to keep. I am not likely to race him myself, and to keep him merely to hack or as a hunter would be an extravagant folly on my part. No, he will have to go, but I am determined that he shall have a good home."

"Do you think that the new viscount may care to purchase him, Miss Karenza?"

"Certainly not!" Karenza's tone was sharp. "I have no wish to be beholdened to a stranger, and one, moreover, who has not shown the slightest concern for our well-being." Then, feeling that she should not express such personal views regarding the new heir, who also was now the agent's employer, she added with a strained smile, "I shall depend on you, Mr Morden, to obtain a good price for Buccaneer. There is no need to hurry over the matter, for the racing stable is fortunately located on the land attached to our inheritance and is therefore outside the domain of the new Lord Darnborough." How hard it was to force those last two words from her lips, but Karenza knew that she must accustom herself to the changes in her circumstances.

Bidding farewell to the old retainer, she turned to make her way back to the house, where her sisters were still busily engaged in transferring their belongings from the main building to the west wing which would now be their home. Karenza was determined that by the time the newcomer arrived to claim his inheritance, there would be little reason for them to meet other than when social obligations made it necessary. For that purpose she had insisted on laying out from their meager funds sufficient monies to pay for the new kitchen and servants' quarters so as to ensure the self-containment of their part of Darnborough Hall. She had even contemplated bricking up the connecting doorway between the west wing and the main house. Only the horrified remonstrances of Mr Ponsonby and the strictures uttered by her devoted Miss Brinton had persuaded her to abandon the exercise, at least for the time being.

Isolated as she had been from the outside world, Karenza had found it impossible to believe that her newly acquired cousin, as heir to the estate, had not been aware of their existence. His failure to attend her father's funeral or acknowledge their sad loss in any way over the past six months had convinced her that he was not only quite unworthy of his good fortune, but was also a cold, selfish, insensitive person, totally unfit to be the guardian of the Coningsby ladies. Oh! If only she had been born a boy, she thought, not for the first time. How different things might have been!

Of the fifth viscount's five daughters, it was Karenza who had been his closest companion, particularly after the death of their mother when the twins were seventeen. Her father had used the lack of a female suitable for guiding his two eldest offspring through the arduous maze of parties, balls, receptions and other events which were the happy lot of young ladies in their first Season in London Society as an excuse to close up his London house. He'd been only too happy to remain year round at his country residence, engrossed in his love of hunting in the winter and racing in the summer. That his family might not share his enjoyment of such rural pursuits apparently was a matter of indifference to the late viscount. But he was not totally unreasonable, and though he refused to countenance a London debut for his two beautiful elder daughters, he raised no objections to their attending the local assemblies or spending a month each year at Harrogate in the company of their mother's sister, Lady Maria Fenestra. Their aunt frequently bewailed the fact that her lovely young nieces lacked the opportunity to make suitable marriages and earnestly regretted the state of her own poor health that made it impossible for her to undergo the rigours of a London Season on their behalf. In response, Karenza would smilingly protest that she had no desire to leave poor papa for such a long time and that Harrogate suited them well enough.

Now, hurrying back from her meeting with the bailiff, Karenza made her way through the small side door of the west wing, hoping to escape a scolding from nurse, who would be only too ready to display her reprobation of the mud clinging to the skirt of her French cambric dress.

"Oh, there you are, my dear Karenza!" It was Miss Brinton, who met her coming along the passage. "I have been looking for you these past ten minutes. I fear that you must be busy but must ask you to bide a while with me."

"What is it, Cousin Brinny? Have the children done anything wrong?" Karenza gave a smiling glance at the short, white-haired figure of her mother's cousin, whom she had persuaded to bear the Misses Coningsby company and to act as their chaperone in order to meet the dictates of polite society. Happily, neither of them found the arrangement irksome. Karenza was genuinely fond of her elderly cousin, who had, in her childhood years, been a kindly mentor on the rare occasions that they met. For her part, Miss Brinton, who had been leading a meagre existence on the pittance left her by her godly but financially unsound father, had been only too happy to exchange her humble dwelling for the comparative luxury of Darnborough Hall.

"No, oh no!" Miss Brinton now hastened to assure Karenza. "I only came to tell you that you have a visitor." She paused to catch her breath. "Sir James is in the blue salon."

"Oh dear, I wonder what brings him here so early in the day. I have not even had time to give cook her instructions." A frown of annoyance crossed Karenza's face, then her natural good manners reasserted themselves. "Brinny dear, be so kind as to tell Sir James that I will be with him shortly. I must go and change first."

"Oh dear, yes, of course I will. So kind of Sir James to come all this way to visit us. You know he is most sincere in his feelings for you, Karenza, and indeed has been informing me of how highly his dear mama regards you." Miss Brinton cast a doubtful look at Karenza's now-amused countenance. "Yes, yes, I know you think him a complete bore. But I do assure you, my love, that there is nothing quite like having a man to lean on. A married woman who can also command the niceties of life is a most fortunate being compared with a single lady, as I well know from personal experience. Pray, do not disregard the advantages which would accrue to you as his wife. I speak, Karenza dear, only for your own good. I hope you are aware that I have your interests close to my heart."

Miss Brinton's tone was becoming quite agitated, and Karenza felt compelled to speak soothingly, assuring her of her awareness of Sir James's worth but then spoiled the effect by adding in a thoughtful voice, "Though I quite agree with you that he would be a kind husband, try as I will, I can't hold him in anything but mild esteem."

"But, my dearest Karenza, you must marry someone. It would not suit you to continue living here, especially once your sisters are wed. And if you wait until that occurs, you will be well and truly on the shelf, and that is not a very happy situation, I promise you." There was a slight tremble to her voice as she spoke these last few words, which touched Karenza's heart. Swiftly she leaned forward and dropped a light kiss on the faded cheek.

"If I do not marry, you shall continue to live with me, if you would. I shan't at all object to having your company instead of Sir James's; indeed, I am convinced that I would much prefer it."

"Oh, you are so kind, so kind to me, my love. I really don't know what to say! I do beg of you, however, to make no decision on the matter for a while. Sir James has too much delicacy of mind to press his suit whilst you are in mourning for your dearest papa. So let us say no more on the subject. You run along and change, whilst I go and keep Sir James company." Then tut-tutting that her cap was all askew, Miss Brinton fled along the passage to assure dear Sir James that her cousin would be happy to receive him shortly.

With a sigh of resignation, Karenza mounted the back staircase leading to the rooms above, her thoughts still on her unwelcome visitor. Sir James, who was little known to the polite world, had but lately succeeded to a modest baronetcy. He had been a quiet, stolid, rather dull little boy who had grown into an equally stolid and rather dull, though worthy, young man. He lacked both wit and liveliness, but prided himself on possession of a great deal of common sense and behaved in the highly punctilious manner of a much older man. His fortune was respectable rather than handsome, but enough to allow him to command the elegancies of life. His estate, which was situated less than fifteen miles from Darnborough Hall, was a snug little property but not, of course, to be compared with the grandeur of the Coningsby residence, even in its present state of neglect. Although always a faithful suitor, Sir James had not pressed his case during the lifetime of the late viscount, uneasily aware that his desire to wed the elder Miss Coningsby might be regarded as presumptuous by her father. The fact that it was his poor seat on a horse which had earned for him his lordship's dislike had not occurred to him. However, the change in the family's circumstances had emboldened him to believe that his suit would now be greatly welcomed. It never entered his mind that Karenza could possibly prefer spinsterhood to marriage to such a worthy fellow as himself.

Karenza allowed herself little time to change, scarcely waiting for her maid to help her step into a most becoming grey figured muslin, unconsciously presenting a picture designed to take any man's breath away. Her figure was elegant, her ankles neat; her complexion had inspired several local admirers to liken it to ripe peaches. A surprisingly firm chin was softened by the exquisite curve of her lips, and delicate high cheekbones set off to perfection the wide green, intelligent eyes, which would occasionally show behind their laughing sparkle a look regarded with some trepidation by her siblings, who knew it betokened some determined line of action from which nothing and no one would deter her. To complete the enchanting appearance, a crown of reddish auburn curls formed a perfect frame to her face. Yet, she seemed unconscious of her charms, and would laughingly decry those who would exclaim at her beauty, begging them not to make jest of her, for everyone knew it had been only their dearest mama who could truly be considered a diamond of the first water.

Scarcely giving herself more than a swift glance in the mirror, Karenza left her room and passed quickly down the stairs to the blue salon, where Sir James was making polite if somewhat laboured conversation with Miss Brinton. Feeling that it behoved her to atone for the length of her delay in coming to meet him, Karenza bestowed on her suitor a warmer smile than was her wont as she went forward to greet him. "How kind of you to call and see how we go on, but you should not have put yourself to so much trouble. I daresay there are many matters requiring your attention elsewhere."

A faint flush of pleasure crept across his stolid but pleasant countenance as Sir James squeezed her hands meaningfully. "Nothing can be of greater importance to me than to put myself at your service, my dear Karenza, although as you so rightly judge, I am a busy man. Yet, you must not suppose that I am neglecting my many duties."

"Am I, then, one of your duties, James?" Karenza's lips were smiling, but there was a slight edge to her voice as she spoke, which caused Miss Brinton to shoot her an imploring glance.

"It remains my dearest wish that my duties could include the care of you and your sisters," he answered so earnestly that Karenza silently chided herself for her impatience with him. Before she could say anything further, he continued in the ponderous tone that always so exasperated her, "Indeed, I would be happy to take your responsibilities onto my own shoulders, for I can only feel that your sisters would benefit from the guidance and advice of an older brother rather than that of a mere . . ." His voice trailed off weakly as he noted the decidedly indignant glint in Karenza's eyes.

" 'That of a mere female,' were you going to say, James?" Karenza asked him acidly, now making no attempt to hide her annoyance.

"I mean no disrespect," he replied hurriedly. "But as my dear mother has often said, there are matters in the rearing of children which need the firm hand of a father."

"What, James! Do you now fancy yourself as a father figure to me and my sisters? Come, come, that won't do, you know. I shall begin to suspect that you had some hidden passion for mama when she was alive. Alas, to think you have been playing me false all these years!" She looked up at him through lowered lashes, trying to prevent herself from laughing at the look of outrage on his face as the implications of her words dawned on him.

His countenance was unbecomingly flushed as he sought to refute her words. "Such levity is most distasteful to me," he said stiffly. "You must be aware that I have nothing but your best interests at heart. I merely wish to alleviate the distress of your position since the death of your poor papa. I am sure you are aware of my regard for you. Were it not for the fact that you are in mourning, I would be hopeful of an alliance being arranged between our two families."

"Your regard for me! An alliance to be arranged! Such passionate utterances leave me totally overwhelmed!" Karenza sank into a chair and hid her laughing face in her hands. Sir James eyed her uncertainly.

"I wish you would not make fun of me!" There was a distinctly petulant note to his voice, and he glanced appealingly at Miss Brinton, who had remained silent throughout these exchanges, no doubt sensing in her an ally to his cause.

Unable to resist the plea in his eyes and determined not to let her young cousin whistle down such an eligible suitor, Miss Brinton sought to pour oil on troubled waters.

"You must forgive Karenza, Sir James," she said, resolutely ignoring the look of reproach from that spirited young lady and the softly spoken *et tu Brute?* which assailed her ears. "It is just that it is difficult for her to adapt to the sudden changes which have occurred of late and the problems involved in the unfortunate delay by the new Lord Darnborough in presenting himself to his cousins and taking up his abode with us."

These latter words unfortunately served only to remind Sir James of yet another grievance. He turned once more to regard that unrepentant damsel with a reproachful eye. "Are you still determined to remove yourselves to the west wing, or have you perhaps considered my advice on the matter and changed your mind?"

"I fear not, my dear James. After all, it was my father who arranged the matter, for which I am most grateful, and I cannot but feel that we should have a greater regard for his wishes than for yours." She met his offended look with one of bland innocence, and there was an uneasy pause before he spoke again.

"Surely by appointing the new viscount as your guardian, your father expected you to remain in his care, at least until you came of age?"

"Not at all. My father had the sense to realise that by leaving us provided with a home we would retain a certain independence which would not otherwise be our lot if we were solely reliant upon the good offices of his heir—especially in view of the size of our fortune, or rather lack of it. As for leaving us in the care of the new viscount, I regret to say that it was merely through papa's lack of sufficient consideration over our future, plus his ignorance of the death of Sir Horace, which has resulted in our present predicament, and not, as you assume, from any desire to see us under the protection of his younger brother."

There was a decidedly militant sparkle in her green eyes as Karenza spoke, and insensitive as he was, even Sir James realised it would ill-suit his cause to press the matter further. Even so, he could not refrain from making one final comment.

"I cannot but disapprove of your actions. It is not suitable for you to deny the rights of your guardian in caring for yourselves. It is undeniably more fitting for him to be in charge of at least the younger girls than for them to reside with you and Sapphira in a separate establishment."

"That is a very stupid thing to say when you must know that Sapphira and I are far more competent to judge our sisters' best interests than any stranger, even one nominally our guardian." There was no hiding her anger at his remark.

"I beg your pardon." Sir James's voice was stiff with resentment. "I did not mean to offend you nor to imply that you were not competent to care for the girls. You have misunderstood my meaning."

"Oh, Karenza dear, I am sure that Sir James has no intention of implying that you are not a suitable person to look after your sisters. Indeed, he has spoken to me this very morning on your loving concern for those sweet creatures." Miss Brinton paused as Karenza rose to her feet, still looking very annoyed. "I know that you cannot like the suggestion that a stranger should have authority over you girls. But, my dear, it is the way of the world that a man should be head of the household. It is merely his protection that Sir James is anxious for you to have, is it not so, sir?"

Sir James regarded the older woman gratefully. "Exactly so, ma'am. I regret if my words have vexed you, Karenza. I did not perhaps express myself suitably, but Miss Brinton has understood my feelings concerning the thought of a helpless female coping with such a lot of responsibility. I must—"

"Oh pray, don't go on in such a way!" begged Karenza. "It is too early in the day to quarrel with you, but I cannot accept what you say. Indeed, we seem to have so little in common in our viewpoints that I am forced to wonder why you persist in holding me in such warm regard." She checked his attempt to interrupt her by laughingly shaking her head. "We won't argue anymore, if you please! I must go now and consult cook and our housekeeper, Mrs Paton, over domestic matters and will not keep you from your duties elsewhere. Thank you for being so kind as to call on us. Pray, convey my sincere regards to your mama. Now I must leave you. Good-bye!"

 3

While Karenza was engaged with the company of her prosing suitor, the Misses Sapphira and Cressidia Coningsby had departed towards the woods in pursuit of Homer, an outsized and shaggy dog of indeterminate parentage, last seen an hour ago in hot chase of cook's favourite cat. Mindful that if anything should happen to cook's darling Toto the family would suffer serious gastronomic deficiencies for an unforeseeable future, both young ladies made all possible speed towards the sounds of faint barking.

"Oh, I do trust that that Homer has not harmed poor little Toto," Sapphira exclaimed in a sweet, soft voice as she peered anxiously ahead.

"For my part, I would be glad to see the last of that horrid creature," her sister countered. "Only yesterday he tore a hole in my best stockings, and when I complained to cook, she said that it was all my fault for teasing him. In fact, I was but playing a game of shuttlecock with Bella." There was a strong note of indignation in Cressidia's voice as she acquainted Sapphira with her unjust treatment.

That they were sisters could be seen, perhaps, in the shape of their faces, but there the resemblance ended. Sapphira Coningsby was as like her twin sister as two guinea pieces. Only those who were extremely well acquainted with the two young women were able to tell them apart. Karenza's eyes were the more lively and intelligent, often glinting with humour as well as kindness, while Sapphira's were more gentle and self-effacing, sometimes rather uncertain. Unlike her older sisters, Cressidia had inherited the dark good looks of her grandmother, possessing an enchantingly pretty face with large hazel eyes, an attractively willful mouth and a surprisingly determined chin. A riot of dark brown curls now peeked out from beneath a becoming straw bonnet which she had donned when they set out to rescue Toto.

The girls' path had now entered the shade of the woods, and the sound of barking grew nearer.

"Homer! Homer!" The girls kept calling, but to little avail; the barking merely increased in volume and intensity.

"Where are you, you stupid animal?" Cressidia called impatiently, while Sapphira cast an anxious eye at the dark shadows of the bushes.

"Oh, there you are, you silly creature!" Cressidia's sharp words were belied by the expression of relief on her face as she ran forward to fasten a leash around the family pet. "Why didn't you come when I called you, you naughty dog!" she scolded. The culprit responded only by frantically waving a plumed tail and refusing to budge from where he stood, his nose pointing towards a vague shape which could be dimly seen lying under one of the bushes.

"Do come along, Cressy dear. We must go—" Sapphira's words ended abruptly at the sound of a low groan nearby. Homer bounded forward, dragging Cressidia after him. She gave a little shriek at the sight of the figure now revealed lying on the ground before her, half-hidden by the shrubs. The next moment Sapphira was at her side. "What is the matter? Have you hurt yourself?" she asked anxiously.

"No, no, but look under that bush! Someone is there! I think that he must be hurt!" Cressidia's voice trembled slightly from the shock of her discovery.

"Quick! Come away! Let's send someone from the house to help him." Sapphira tugged at her sister's arm while Homer only increased the volume of his barking as the groans continued.

"No, Sapphira! We cannot leave the poor soul thus with no one else here. Let us see what is wrong with him." Disregarding her sister's protests that it might be some dangerous villain lying in wait for them, Cressidia, whose eyes were now accustomed to the dark shadows of the undergrowth, saw that the shape was that of a young man lying on one side.

"Come, Sapphira, we must help him, for I fear he may be badly hurt." Another groan seemed to bear out her words. Touched by the stranger's obvious need for their help, Sapphira overcame her initial reluctance and knelt by her sister's side. Together, they turned the man onto his back.

His face was alarmingly pale. Not really sure of what she was doing, Cressidia slipped an arm under his head, raised it gently and placed it on her lap. For the first time they could see him clearly. A hawkish nose and a wide, humorous mouth were his most noticeable features. His chestnut locks were matted with dried blood, and his breathing was laboured.

Cressidia raised frightened eyes to her sister. "Do you think he is going to die? Oh, we must get help for him immediately." As she spoke, she lay his arm, which was dangling awkwardly at his side, across his chest and loosened his neatly tied neckcloth.

Sapphira, whose natural compassion had overcome her fears, lay a soft hand on his chest. "His heart seems to be beating fairly strongly, but I agree that the sooner we get a doctor for him, the better. Come, Cressy, let us return home at once and send the men down to fetch this poor creature."

"I can't leave him here all alone," Cressidia protested. "You go at once, and I'll await your return here. Don't let us waste time in arguing. My mind is made up. Homer can stay to protect me."

Persuaded as much by the alarming pallor of the young man as by her sister's words, Sapphira rose reluctantly to her feet. With a last worried backward glance, and the unnecessary admonition to her sibling not to stir from where she was, Sapphira departed at a rapid pace, wondering as she went if she was indeed right to leave her sister alone with the injured stranger.

Once Sapphira was out of sight, Cressidia began to wonder how she could best help the injured man. "What a pity I have no brandy with me," she murmured to herself, recalling her father's fondness for this potation and his firm belief in its effectiveness as a cure to all ills.

"I wish so, too."

Cressidia gave a little shriek of surprise at the softly spoken words. "Oh, you're feeling better! I'm so glad!" she exclaimed delightedly as she bent over him, her fingers unconsciously stroking the tangled, matted locks away from his face. She found herself gazing into dazed-looking brown eyes which regarded her with puzzled astonishment.

"Who are you?" His voice was low and uncertain. Cressidia's smile of relief at his apparent recovery was dazzling, and a look of pure wonder crossed his face.

"I'm Cressidia Coningsby," she answered a little shyly. She paused a moment before asking, "And what is your name?"

A puzzled frown creased his brow, and horror slowly dawned in the brown eyes as he gazed despairingly up at her. "I don't know. Oh, my God, I don't know who I am!" He gave a deep groan and lifted a weak, shaking hand to his head, wincing as he touched the swollen, bloody contusion behind his right ear.

"Pray, do not concern yourself over your loss of memory. 'Tis probably but a momentary affair, for you have suffered a severe blow to your head and no doubt your wits are temporarily confused. Just rest quietly, for help is on its way." But her patient only responded to her reassuring words with a long moan.

"Oh please, sir, do not die!" Cressidia almost wailed the words as she loosened his shirt and felt once more for his heartbeat, while at her side, Homer threw back his head and uttered a dismal howl of sympathy. A tear made its way down Cressidia's cheek as she regarded the handsome, young head resting on her lap. Oh, to think how much she had longed for romance and adventure. Now that it had come upon her, all she could do was to weep. Pah! She should be ashamed of herself. Mentally she chided herself for her weakness and looked around for something to occupy her mind until the longed-for help arrived. Perhaps there was something near to hand which would help her to establish the identity of the stranger. Feeling a little guilty, she slid a hand into the pockets of his coat, but they yielded her nothing. She subconsciously noted the fine texture of the cloth, the well-cut buckskin breeches and what once no doubt had been gleaming topboots. A gentleman of quality, she'd decided, but not one of the dandy set, for no corset hugged his waist or absurd high-pointed collar his neck. Somehow this knowledge pleased her. Her eyes passed beyond his figure, taking in the imprint of horses hooves nearby and the surrounding soft ground of mud and leaves, seeking in some way to account for the accident which had befallen him.

It must have been nearly three quarters of an hour later when Homer suddenly pricked up his ears and gave a few short, excited barks. Cressidia turned her head in the direction the hound was looking and listened intently. Very faintly she could hear the sound of her name being called over and over again. A feeling of relief swept over her.

"I'm here!" she shouted and then cast an anxious glance at the unconscious figure whose head still remained resting in her lap. He showed no reaction to the noise, and a note of fear entered her voice as she called out again, "I'm over here, over here! Do hurry please!" Then she promptly burst into tears of relief as she saw the familiar figure of Karenza hurrying towards her.

"Come, Cressy darling, let me relieve you of your burden."

How glad Cressidia was to hear her sister's familiar tone, though strangely reluctant to have the brown curly head lifted from her lap. She cast another lingering look at the still-unconscious figure before raising anxious eyes to Karenza, who knelt in front of her, her hands already holding a dampened cloth with which she carefully wiped the mud and blood from the young man's injured head.

"Do you think he will die, Karenza?" Cressidia wailed.

Her sister shot her a surprised look before answering compassionately. "He has suffered an unpleasant injury, but not one that appears to be beyond help, though I think we should get him to a warm place as soon as possible; he feels very cold to the touch." As she spoke, she stared down at the young man's visage and a puzzled look crossed her face. "How odd!" she exclaimed. "I have the feeling that I know him, yet I can swear that we have never met. Still, that's not at all important at the moment. Ned, bring the blanket here and wrap the young man in it. Be careful now, how you move him!" she added sharply.

Cressidia became aware of the numbers of people milling around her. A couple of footmen and two of the stablehands gently lifted the inanimate figure onto the blanket. Then taking a corner each, they moved carefully forward along the path with their burden, Sapphira's gentle voice urging them to take care not to jolt the unconscious figure.

"We shall have to look after him until his memory returns," Cressidia stated firmly, determined not to be parted from the fascinating young man. "The poor man has no recollection of who he is or where he comes from. It would be positively heartless to abandon him in such a sorry state."

Karenza considered this statement thoughtfully, knitting her brows as she wrestled with its implications.

"Where shall we put him?" Cressidia's voice interrupted her thoughts.

"I am not sure," Karenza answered slowly. "We cannot put him in the west wing with only ourselves there, yet we no longer have the right to offer him the hospitality of the hall."

"But we can't turn him away!" Cressidia sounded aghast at the prospect of losing her patient.

"I know," said Karenza decisively. "We'll put him in one of the upper floor guest rooms in the old hall. Our new cousin does not seem highly desirous of making our acquaintance, so I daresay that the young man will recover and be gone long before the sixth viscount condescends to visit us."

Cressidia regarded her solemnly. "I believe that it is not simply a case of caring for this poor man until he is recovered from his injuries."

Karenza turned her head to look at her, her expressive eyes questioning.

"I feel I should warn you," Cressidia continued earnestly, "that our actions may involve us in some danger."

Karenza's face reflected her astonishment at these words. "Danger? For us? Pray, what do you mean, Cressy dear?" A hint of laughter had entered her voice.

"The blow to the young man's head—it was no accident." The calm certainty in Cressidia's voice was impressive. "I looked most carefully for signs of a stone or rock or anything that could have been responsible for such a wound, but there was nothing in the vicinity of his fall to account for it."

"Perhaps his horse kicked him after he had been thrown."

"No! Two horses had stood still at the point where he fell. Their marks are clear to read. It is obvious to me that he was deliberately attacked."

Every member of the late viscount's family had been brought up with a detailed knowledge of horses, and following their tracks had been a favourite childhood game. Karenza had no doubt that what her sister said was true. Still, there could be many innocent explanations for the accident, which would no doubt come to light when the stranger recovered consciousness. Having no desire to spoil her younger sister's romantic adventure by uttering such prosaic thoughts, Karenza assured her in a suitably grave voice that she would indeed be on her guard against any dastardly person who might seek to inflict any further injury on their helpless guest.

At this point they were relieved to find themselves back at the hall, and they ascended to the upper bedroom. Karenza directed the men to gently lay the young man on the bed which she had directed be prepared for him before she left. Then she and nurse carefully eased off his coat and began to remove the bloodstained shirt beneath, while Cressidia hovered anxiously at her side. With her usual quiet competence, Miss Brinton came in carefully carrying a bowl of warm water and some cloths.

"I sent young Jason for dear Doctor Beech, as you requested, my dear Karenza. I expect he will be here at any moment," she said, carefully placing the bowl on the small sidetable as she spoke and smiling reassuringly as she caught Cressidia's anxious gaze. "It is fortunate I remembered that it is his morning for calling upon our rector. He has no more than three miles to come."

"Then, we need do no more than prepare his patient for his examination," said Karenza in a calm voice, and leaned forward to help nurse as she eased the shirt off the unconscious figure, but her expression changed suddenly as she did so. "He's been shot!" she exclaimed incredulously as she stared down at the gaping wound in the stranger's shoulder, almost unable to believe her eyes.

"I told you that it was no accident that befell him," announced Cressidia in a satisfied tone before clasping her hands together and adding faintly, "Oh, who could wish to kill such a handsome young man?"

The tumult of their thoughts were broken into by Sapphira's soft voice. "I have brought you my sal volatile, Karenza dear. Perhaps it may be of some help to the poor fellow."

"Indeed, yes." Karenza took it eagerly, then after a momentary hesitation, handed it to Cressidia. "Pray, my dear, hold it under his nose and see if it will help him."

Cressidia seized the little bottle and not unwillingly slipped her arm under the brown, curly head, raising it up against her shoulder as she waved the hartshorn gently beneath his nose. His eyelids fluttered and opened. Confused eyes blinked uncomprehendingly at the face bending over him. His gaze wandered past to encompass Karenza and Sapphira and behind them the butler's square countenance, which exuded his disapproval at such goings-on in a nobleman's household.

"Where the devil am I?" the injured man asked in a faint, puzzled tone. A look of vague recognition dawned as his glance fell once more on Cressidia's anxious face. He noted the tear sparkling on her cheek and spoke gently to her, "Don't cry, my angel! I promise you that I shall not die!"

"But who attacked you?" Cressidia burst forth, unable to contain her thoughts any longer.

He moved slightly and grimaced with the pain. "Ma'am, I know not who I am or how I came to be here. My mind is a complete blank, but . . ." With a shaking hand he found her fingers and raised them to his lips. "I am more than happy to be with you and only wish . . ." Here his words broke off and his head lolled back into Cressidia's arms. With a cry of alarm, she eased him gently onto the pillow, but before anyone could speak, a familiar figure made his appearance in the doorway.

"Now, now, what have we here, Miss Karenza?" The brisk tones of Dr Beech had a comforting ring to them, and the ladies turned to him in a welter of explanations. The shrewd blue eyes of the doctor twinkled benignly as he raised a hand to check the flow of words. "Perhaps it would be better if I were to examine my patient first, and you can tell me all you know about him later."

Grateful for his commonsense approach to the matter, Karenza smiled her acquiescence and moved to assist him in laying bare the young man's injured shoulder.

"We think he has been shot," she said calmly.

Pursing his lips, the doctor bent to examine his patient more closely before opening his bag and bringing out some rather nasty-looking instruments, at the sight of which Cressidia gave a violent shudder. In a faint voice, she informed her sisters that she would go in search of some basilicum powder and bandages, for they would no doubt have need of them.

It was some time before Cressidia returned, and by then the operation to remove the ball from the wounded man's shoulder was over. Thankfully, Cressidia was able to take her place by his side once more without losing her composure.

Speedily the doctor bound the injured man's shoulder and then carefully investigated his other wounds before pronouncing himself satisfied with his handiwork. Almost as though he had heard the doctor's words, the stranger slowly opened his eyes. The gaze he bestowed on his anxious custodians was one of total incomprehension. Only the sight of Cressidia sitting beside him seemed to bring him some relief. He regarded her with an almost desperate expression in his eyes.

"Oh, pray, don't leave me! I don't know who or where I am, but you are my guardian angel. Do not leave me, I beg of you!" No one present could be left untouched by the pathos of his words, and none demurred when Cressidia swore that nothing would tear her from his side.

By next morning the household had recovered its equilibrium. Cressidia had refused to be parted from her own special protegé. Happily, Cousin Brinny's soft heart had yielded to her charge's urgent pleas, and with surprising forbearance, she had taken turns with nurse to act as chaperone during the many hours Cressidia spent at the young man's bedside.

Over the next three days he made excellent progress so far as his injuries were concerned, which were less severe than had been feared, but his memory remained as blank as ever.

"I know what to do," Cressidia said firmly on the morning of the third day when her patient showed signs of acute depression over his failure to recall his past. "I shall go through every man's name I know and as I say each one, you might possibly recognise your own."

The young man looked at her hopefully. "Would you really do so? If I could but remember just my Christian name, I would feel so much better."

"Then I will begin with all the names I can think of starting with *A* and work my way through the alphabet," she said determinedly.

The brown eyes sparkled at her. "That is an excellent idea, for you cannot marry a man whose name you do not know."

"Oh hush!" Cressidia shot a worried glance at Miss Brinton, who was snoozing gently in her chair. Satisfied that she was not listening to their conversation, Cressidia turned her attention once more to the reclining figure beside her. She gave him a delighted smile. "Do you really want to marry me? How romantic!"

He raised his head from the pillows. "I forbid you to marry anyone except me."

"Are you proposing to me?" Cressidia asked rapturously.

"Of course I am, but I cannot approach your family on the matter until I know my name and background."

"Well then," said Cressidia in a very practical tone, "we must solve that problem as quickly as we can. Let us start at once." She took a deep breath. "Now listen very carefully and stop me as soon as a name sounds familiar to you. Now then, let me think . . . Adam, Adolphus, Artemis, Arthur . . ." Her voice carried on with remorseless regularity. After half an hour she was beginning to regret her suggestion, but each time she paused, a pair of beseeching eyes would gaze up at her and she would continue. By the time she had reached *J* her voice was becoming a little hoarse, yet she ploughed on gamely. "Jessamy, James, Jason, John, Jonathan, Joshua . . ."

"Stop! That's it!" The voice from the bed was excited.

"Joshua?" Cressidia felt disappointed; it was not a very romantic name, she thought.

"No! Not Joshua, Jonathan! That's my name—Jonathan." He repeated the name with great satisfaction.

Cressidia clapped her hands with delight. "Oh, Jonathan! Why, that is one of my favourite names. How clever of you to be called by it. I must go and tell the others the good news." She leapt to her feet and was gone, almost dancing down the stairs with delight at the news she bore. She found Karenza in the blue salon, frowning over a letter she was reading.

"Karenza, Karenza, his name is Jonathan—he has remembered it—is it not wonderful?" She was calling out her news as she skipped happily towards Karenza, her face flushed with pleasure and excitement.

Karenza gave a sigh of relief. "That is good news, my dear, and very welcome, too, for I have just received a letter from our new cousin informing us that he will call on us this coming Thursday, or so I believe it says. His writing is a shocking scrawl and difficult to read. I am therefore more than glad to hear that our unfortunate guest will be able to return to his own family before then. How relieved they will be to have news of him!"

"Oh, but it is only his Christian name that he remembers. It is Jonathan. Such a nice name, do you not think?"

"No more than that?" Karenza sounded agitated. "How provoking! Come what may, he will have to leave us soon. I cannot bring myself to ask any favours of our father's heir, and certainly not one which could well merit his censure, for he sounds a most odiously cold-hearted creature. He has written me the curtest of notes, making no apology for his neglect of us."

"Well, we've another six days before his arrival, and who knows, by then Jonathan may well have discovered his full name," Cressidia said stoutly, determined to keep Jonathan with her until he was fully recovered. "And if not, then we shall have to find some place to hide him. It should not be for long, for I do not think that our horrid cousin will remain with us for many days."

"Yes, that is the impression he has given me," stated Karenza dryly. "Indeed, he seems strangely loath to visit us at all. Were it not for the sake of the estate's tenants, I would wish he did not come! Still, we can no doubt survive the dubious honour of his presence for what I assume will be but a fleeting visit. Now we must tell the others our news." Then with their arms entwined affectionately, the two sisters made their way to the west wing.

4

It was perhaps inevitable that the long-awaited news of the prospective visit by the new heir should swiftly reach the ears of the village of Upper Tilling and its surrounding farms and estates. Throughout this small community much speculation ensued.

No one was actually acquainted with the new viscount, but several ladies had, on various occasions, spent some weeks in London and now recalled that they had, in fact, seen him in the park or at the opera. His reputation as one of the leaders of the ton, a regular non pareil, and in the eyes of many a would-be young blade, an out-and-out top sawyer, served to heighten their excitement.

Ironically enough, the object of all this much interest, together with his good-looking nephew, now made his entrance upon the local scene almost unnoticed. This was not due to any deliberate action on his part but rather to the sad mishap of one of his lordship's horses having cast a shoe, thus requiring the two men to proceed at a much more stately pace than was their wont.

It was almost dark by the time a well-sprung chaise, with a coat of arms emblazoned on its side, and carrying two impatient and hungry gentlemen made its way slowly under the archway of the King's Head Inn and came to a standstill in the courtyard beyond. A lounging postboy, leaning against a wall chewing a straw, showed little sign of interest at their arrival, and it was not until Lord Darnborough thrust open the door of the chaise and sprang down, closely followed by Justin Mapping, that he reluctantly came forward to enquire of their needs. After a brief colloquy, the boy disappeared in the direction of the stables, while Lord Darnborough and his nephew made their way towards the stout innkeeper peering from the inn doorway. Behind them two servants made haste to off-load their luggage.

Soon aware that he beheld none other than the new Lord Darnborough, the landlord was overwhelming him with offers of all the comforts of his abode, including the best bedchamber for his lordship; the younger man found himself allocated a small, rather noisy back room overlooking the courtyard.

It was not long before Justin rejoined his relative in the comfort of a snug little parlour, where a small fire fought off the faint chill of the September night. Here he strongly voiced his protests.

"Dash it, Marcus, it's all very well for you to decide to spend the night here instead of going on to the Hall, but I declare I shan't sleep a wink in that bed. It has more lumps than the cobblestone yard!"

"Pray, accept my apologies for your unfortunate situation." There was an amused note in his lordship's voice as he eyed his indignant companion. "But I'm afraid we could scarce expect to be received very graciously if we presented ourselves at the Hall at this late hour. Besides, they will have already dined, and I'm damned if I wish to wait much longer for a meal."

No words could have appealed more strongly to his nephew, now reminded of his own pangs of hunger. "By

George, you're right! I'm absolutely famished. It will be too bad if we should not be well fed after all our troubles."

Justin's fears proved groundless, and it was not too long before their host was spreading before them a repast calculated to appeal to the most jaded appetite. There was a silence as the two men appreciatively worked their way through ducks with bechamel sauce, some tarragons joined by a dish of buttered spinach and a large mutton pie, followed by a healthy wedge of apple pie and savoy cake. All washed down by an excellent burgundy. Not for nothing had the landlord's good lady been assistant cook in a gentleman's London residence for many years before bestowing her talents as well as her ample figure upon the fortunate Ned Haggard, innkeeper.

A hand or two of piquet helped to while away the next few hours, during which time Justin sought to persuade his uncle his urgent need of marriage to the lovely Maria of the gaming club, but to little avail. Then the two gentlemen prepared to retire. My Lord Darnborough to ponder, with some distaste, on the duties he would assume on the morrow, while his nephew reflected sadly on the hardhearted attitude of the one person he had expected to support his suit.

It was the viscount rather than the young Mr Mapping who woke early the next morning. Pulling back the curtains that encircled the four-poster, he retrieved his watch from under the pillows. The early hour it denoted caused him to utter a groan and sink back in an attempt to recapture sleep. Outside could be heard the clatter of pails and the voices of stablelads teasing the maids and the latter's laughing protests. Finally surrendering to the inevitable, the viscount cast off the bedclothes and shortly was making his way to the stables, which were situated at the far end of the courtyard. His nephew continued to sleep soundly in spite of his earlier forebodings.

The day was fresh and fair, a morning mist still shrouded the distance as his lordship swung himself up on the hired horse and rode out of the yard. The main road through the village soon took him into open countryside. Anxious to leave the deeply rutted highway behind him, the viscount turned off to follow a narrow track which ran through a tangle of brambles and trees.

He was not to be the only early riser that morning, for Karenza had already emerged from the house in search of the wild herbs that cook had demanded for the very special repast to be set before the new heir the following day. Conscious of the need to preserve her clothes, now that their replacement could no longer be assured, Karenza had donned a somewhat ancient dimity from her wardrobe. It was a trifle old-fashioned, and its original green had faded to a rather indeterminate hue. A stout pair of shoes clad her feet and a sunbonnet completed her outfit. Carrying a large basket, she made her way through the woods, beyond which lay the five-acre field where Will, the cowman, had assured her she would find the very herbs and berries that cook needed. As usual, her companion was Homer, who bounded joyfully ahead in his happy and rumbustious fashion, every now and then dashing back to his mistress to ensure himself of her whereabouts before rushing off once more in futile pursuit of some startled pheasant or rabbit.

Karenza never concerned herself over the fact that she went unescorted. She had developed this habit in order to escape the noise and demands of her younger sisters as well as their plaintively protesting governess, Miss Denny, who was more than grateful now-a-days to find her charges reduced to just dear Arabella and Drusilla.

As she walked, Karenza was, however, aware of an overwhelming sense of depression. Soon, all too soon, she would no longer have automatic right of entry to the house that had been her home for so long. Oh, it was likely that the new heir would not require her to remain within the confines of the west wing; indeed, it was probable that he would not wish her to reside there at all, not that she would take any notice of his desires in that respect. No, the problem was that she no longer would be mistress of Darnborough Hall, but merely tolerated as an unwanted appendage, and she knew it was not in her character to take easily to such a situation. She realised she had to accept the fact that her old home had a new owner, but the pain of that acceptance would remain with her. From that there was no escape.

Immersed in her sad thoughts, she was scarcely aware of the tears trickling down her cheeks as she made her way into the shadows of the old beech woods, through which a rough path led to the five-acre field. Blindly her feet followed the familiar track until the unexpected sound of galloping hooves captured her attention. It was perhaps unfortunate that at that very moment Homer should have put up a rabbit and pursued it with yelping enthusiasm as it ran straight down the track into the path of the oncoming horseman. There was a sharp expletive and frantic yelps as horse, dog and man became one confused tangle. The rabbit, making the most of his opportunity, departed with alacrity.

Karenza ran forward, arriving at the scene just in time to see the horse stumble and deposit its rider in a patch of briars before taking further fright and bolting off down the track, its reins flapping wildly and loose stirrups pounding its heaving sides. The beast was soon lost from sight.

A muttered curse reassured Karenza as she peered anxiously at the figure attempting to detach itself from the brambles that entwined his arms and legs.

"I trust you are not hurt, sir?" she said gently as the tall man finally regained his feet and moved towards her.

"And what do you mean by letting that misbegotten cur attack my horse!" His voice showed a sad lack of respect for the presence of a lady, and there was little doubt that he was extremely angry.

Karenza eyed him speculatively, aware that his anger was due more to injured dignity than physical pain. Still, he should not address her in such a rude manner.

"I must apologise if my dog upset you, but although he may have startled your horse, it was not really his fault that you fell off!" Her tone indicated all too clearly her low opinion of his riding abilities, and for one who was admired as a fearless horseman, who hunted with the Quorn and was regarded as a top-of-the-trees rider by his contemporaries, the experience was a salutary one. There was a stunned silence, then his lordship gave a short bark of laughter as he came closer to her. Karenza regarded him with a candid stare; he was a most striking-looking man, quite unlike anyone in her immediate circle. She lifted her face to him, causing his brows to rise in pleased surprise at her enchanting countenance. Fearing her words may have left him a trifle abashed, she addressed him more kindly. "Since you do not seem much hurt, I shall leave you. If you wish to rest here a while, I will arrange for someone to catch your horse and return it to you."

A cool smile curled his lips. "Fair maiden, you have rendered me horseless and as much bruised in my feelings as in my body. You therefore owe me recompense. Come, give me a kiss for my pains!"

Before she could rebuke him for his forwardness—for never before had anyone addressed her in such a manner— he had his arm around her, and she found herself being ardently kissed. Karenza went scarlet with fury and fought strenuously to free herself from his restraining arms. With her eyes spitting fire, she managed to wrench herself loose, panting with rage. But instead of taking to her heels as any sensible girl would have done, she dealt her attacker a stinging blow across the ear, which caused his head to ring. Before she could repeat her action, he tightly seized her wrist in his hand.

"Tut, tut, my dear! You should be flattered by my attentions, or are you playing hard to get!"

Karenza went rigid with temper, her cheeks still aflame. "Why you, you pestilential knave, you pox on humanity!" she said chokingly. "How dare you treat me like some bit of Covent Garden muslin!" The words were out before she could stop them.

Her assailant burst out laughing. "Bravo! And where did my fine lady learn such expressions? Shame on you!"

Karenza, who suddenly realised just what she had said, stopped, somewhat aghast at having given such free range to her tongue. Then realising he was only tormenting her, she answered in a spirited tone, "It is your behaviour that is abominable! I shall tell you plainly, sir, that you are no gentleman! Kindly remove yourself from my vicinity."

"I have no intention of doing that, at least not yet. Tell me, who are you? I took you for some village lass."

"Oh, did you! Well, I can tell you that if you think that is the way you can conduct yourself in this part of the country, you will find yourself in danger of having a pitchfork stuck through you."

"From your tone you sound as if you would approve of the idea," he commented dryly.

"I do," Karenza stated frankly, "in fact, I would very much like to see you on the wrong end of a pitchfork."

"Come, forgive me," the stranger said coaxingly. "I'll even apologise for my behaviour if it upset you, for I vow you are a most unusual female."

"How deeply flattered I am," Karenza said with withering sarcasm. "I daresay I should be quite overcome by your words if I had any care for your opinion, but since my only desire is never to see you again, I really cannot succumb to your charm."

"Spiteful little devil." The viscount's eyes glinted appreciatively. "How was I to recognise the fact you are a lady, dressed as you are and roaming the countryside unescorted, with not even a maid to accompany you."

"Oh my, such chivalry! I find your utterances quite overwhelming. Pray, do tell me, are you so lacking the ability to retain the affections of a lady of your own class that you must pursue innocent country maidens!" Karenza enquired sweetly.

"That's enough of that, my girl!" The laughter was gone from his voice, and the grey eyes had lost all trace of humour.

Karenza, glad to see her words had struck home, was determined to punish him further. "I suppose that once a man reaches your years, he finds consolation in making unwanted attacks on defenceless females." She looked at his stunned expression with bland innocence. "Why, I can well imagine you as the sort of person who . . . who kisses the housemaid under the stairs."

He was so thunderstruck by her words that he let go of her wrist. "A man of my . . . of my years! Oh, my God! Kiss the housemaid under the stairs. Why you abominable—" He broke off as he saw the irresistible mirth bubble up in her green eyes. "All right. I truly beg your pardon. You have most definitely put me in my place!" He stopped abruptly as Homer decided to include him in a frenzy of affectionate greetings after returning from his futile pursuit of his lordship's horse.

"Sit!" commanded the viscount. Recognising the voice of command, Homer gave a final apologetic lick before rolling over on his back and waving four muddy, furry legs in the air. His lordship absentmindedly bent down to scratch the stomach of the now-ecstatic hound.

"How is it that your father permits you to wander without a chaperone?" he demanded curtly.

"I have no father," she answered shortly.

"Well then, what about your brother or guardian?" the viscount enquired impatiently, frowning at some hidden thought.

"I am thankful to say that I have been spared the tribulations of a brother, and as for my guardian, you need have no fear of him," Karenza said bitterly.

"Oh, why not?" His lordship was amused and intrigued by the note of censure in her voice.

She brushed a red curl back from her forehead, and her eyes gleamed with dislike as she spoke. "He is an elderly, cold-hearted man who is too self-centered to concern himself with what he would no doubt consider a trivial affair." The viscount looked somewhat taken back by the vehemence of her words. "So you need have no fear of someone calling you out for your disgraceful behaviour," she added acidly. "Besides, he is not expected to be with us until tomorrow, so you have time anyway to make your escape."

The viscount flushed angrily at her words. "I'll have you know I fear no man, and I should box your ears for even suggesting it."

"Well, you can't expect me to acknowledge your bravery. After all, my only experience in your company has shown me that you have few if any scruples against pressing your attentions on a helpless female!"

"Not all that helpless," his lordship said ruefully, rubbing his ear. "Come, let us not quarrel. I admit I behaved badly, but I must now try to atone for my misdeeds. I cannot leave you to walk through these wood all alone."

"Oh, I shall be quite safe once you have gone," Karenza said affably.

"Little vixen," he murmured appreciatively. "I feel that your guardian should receive my commiserations for what must be a most onerous duty." He fell into step beside her as she turned to make her way back along the track, glancing curiously at the lovely face, reluctant somehow to be parted from her. "Pray, do tell me where you live, unless the thought frightens you."

"What a stupid suggestion," she said scornfully, "as though I would be afraid of such an idiotic creature as yourself knowing where I reside." Secretly Karenza found herself rather attracted to the handsome stranger, and as she glanced up at him, through lowered lashes, she was aware that she would not be adverse to seeing him again. They had reached the stile by now, and as the stranger assisted her over it, she found herself thrilling to his touch, and her voice took on a slight breathlessness as she spoke. "I will say good-bye to you now, sir, as I live quite nearby. You can see our chimneys over yonder, just above the trees." She dropped him a slight curtsey.

"Let it be au revoir, not good-bye, for I expect to be in this area for some time and would be happy to renew our acquaintanceship." There was an oddly serious note to his voice which surprised even himself.

"That will certainly make life more interesting, for we have been sadly lacking in amusing scandals of late!" she commented lightly.

"I see that I shall have to try to revive my shocking reputation. But before I leave you, pray inform me of your name, my sweet delight."

Curbing a strong desire to linger further and listen to more of such pleasurable nonsense, Karenza took her basket, sadly devoid of its promised herbs, from her companion. Rather shyly she raised glowing eyes to his.

"I am Miss Coningsby of Darnborough Hall," she said simply.

"Oh, my God!" There was no mistaking the shock in his voice.

Misunderstanding it, Karenza allowed herself a brief smile at his obvious discomfort at discovering her identity.

"And you?" She cast him an enquiring look.

"Marcus . . ." he hesitated, undecided whether to reveal his relationship to her. Before he could commit himself further, she had turned from him, giving her dress a little shake.

"Good-bye, Mr Marcus," she called smilingly over her shoulder. "I do hope you find your horse again soon." And before he could utter another word, she was gone, leaving him staring after her, more disconcerted than he could recall being in all of his thirty-two years.

Slowly and pensively he wended his way back down the track, scarcely aware of the half-hour trudge to the highway. No sign of his horse could be seen, and he had just about resigned himself to the tedium of the long walk back to the inn when he heard the sound of cantering hooves. With a hearty sigh of relief, he saw the familiar figure of his nephew astride a large, clumsy-looking chestnut, leading another horse by his side.

"Marcus! Thank God you're safe! What a fright you gave us." Justin's anxious eyes took in his uncle's somewhat crumpled condition and a smile twitched the corners of his mouth. "Oh no, not you, Marcus, taking a toss like the veriest clodpole!"

"Cease your drivel, halfling!" his lordship said amiably. "The brute stumbled when a dog ran across its path and we parted company. I am, I must admit, more than glad to see you."

"Well, when your horse came galloping back to its stable, all of a lather and no sign of you, I feared the worse. Having no idea of the direction you had taken, I've had half the countryside out looking for you."

"The devil you have!" Darnborough looked rather taken back by these words.

"Oh yes," his nephew rattled on with increasing good humour. "And a mighty fine joke they found it, to be looking for the new viscount in every ditch between here and the next county. 'Twas lucky some worthy fellow mentioned seeing fresh horse's tracks coming from this direction, otherwise you would have had a long walk!"

"Did you have to say who I was?" his lordship groaned in dismay.

Justin shot him an understanding look. "They already knew it, no doubt the inn's ostler spread the news of your identity. I expect they'll be talking about nothing else for the next week or so," he added cheerfully.

Lord Darnborough, who felt he had borne enough for one day, commanded his young relative to spare him any further comment on his mishap and instead turn his mind on how to occupy himself for another day based in their present abode, as they would not be presenting themselves at the Hall until the morrow.

Justin raised astonished eyes to his uncle and demanded to know the reason for this change of plan. Unwilling yet to discuss the events of the morning, Lord Darnborough regarded him coolly. "You may say it is merely a whim."

"The devil it is!" Justin answered indignantly. "What has happened to you this morning to bring about this change of mind? Your fall has not affected your brain?" he asked anxiously.

"Well, I think it may have influenced my decision," the viscount conceded, endeavouring to keep the laughter from his voice.

"I don't understand it, but I'll allow you to know best," Justin stated magnanimously, before adding in a brighter tone, "I hear there is to be a mill in Kimbolton this afternoon. 'Tis but three miles from the village. Would you care to accompany me there, since we must pass the time somehow?"

"I should consider it a privilege," his lordship said blandly as they once more entered the courtyard of the inn and prepared to dismount. "Now I shall leave you to make the necessary explanations and to dispense largesse on my behalf while I go and change. Do try and rescue something of my reputation as a horseman in the process."

 5

Karenza made her way slowly home, her thoughts in a quite unaccustomed turmoil. Considering she had undergone a most agitating experience, she could not understand why she did not feel more indignant or upset. Indeed, there was a lightness of spirit within her which was almost disconcerting. Undoubtedly her encounter with a man who was quite clearly a rake and who in addition had committed the gross impropriety of kissing her against her will should have left her if not in a swoon, then at least in a disturbed state of mind. Certainly, she had not enjoyed being imprisoned in his arms nor the rough way he had tilted her face to bring his lips forcefully against hers.

Yet there had been one mad moment when she had known an urge to respond, and there had been a most unusual stirring in her body, which excited and disturbed her. After such treatment she should not have lingered to exchange words with her attacker, and certainly to have boxed his ears in such an unladylike manner had been an act of madness. Yet, she did not regret it, nor his kisses, either, a small voice within softly added.

How could she think thus! Of course she had disliked his attentions. Yet, Karenza wondered if the hot-blooded actions of the stranger were not more to her liking than the cold-blooded sobriety of her would-be suitor, Sir James.

The veriest thought of James acting so passionately brought a smile to her lips, and she knew then that she could never accept him as her husband; the rude, arrogant and over-powering stranger had helped make up her mind on that score.

Karenza was unsure whether or not to inform Sapphira of her experience, for it would be difficult to explain why she should wish to see the outrageous Mr Marcus again if he made good his promise to renew their acquaintanceship. It was highly unlikely that he would be so shameless as to refer to it himself on making his bow to her sisters, yet it would be necessary for them to know she had already met the man, since there could be little other reason for him to call on her at the Hall. Then she thought that the likeliest probability was that Mr Marcus had no real intention in prolonging his stay in the village and therefore there was really no point in mentioning the matter to anyone. Thus firmly dismissing him from her thoughts, Karenza reentered her home.

It was decided the next day to await the arrival of their guardian in the great salon leading off the entrance hall of the main house; therefore dinner that evening would be served in the vast dining hall in all its splendour. At first Karenza had been inclined to insist on receiving the viscount as her guest in the west wing, but eventually the protestations of Miss Brinton had made her see it as being an unnecessarily hostile gesture towards her guardian and convinced her it would be more dignified and clearly illustrate her undoubted competence as hostess of the former viscount's household to receive his lordship in more formal surroundings.

Overcoming the objections of Miss Brinton and Miss Denny, all five of the Honourable Misses Coningsby were assembled in the great salon by four o'clock in anticipation of his lordship's arrival. Chaperoned by the two elderly ladies, Karenza had the dubious satisfaction of knowing that the presence of seven females would have a daunting effect on any solitary male. In fact, the young ladies presented a very charming picture as they dispersed themselves amidst the grandeur of the old room. Arabella, under threat of dire consequences should she misbehave in any way, was a somewhat subdued figure, with her head bent over her sampler and an unusually thoughtful frown of concentration on her face. Beside her, Drusilla sorted her embroidery silks, pausing now and then to discuss the perplexing question of selecting the right shades for her design with her preceptress, Miss Denny, who kept a watchful eye on her two charges.

Miss Brinton moved to seat herself by the window, where she resumed her knitting, while Sapphira carefully perused the latest fashions in the ladies journal, pausing occasionally to comment on her findings to Cressidia reclining alongside her, who was unsuccessfully wrestling with her tatting. Only Karenza seated near the centre of the room, gazing down at her tightly clenched hands, was unoccupied and apparently immersed in her thoughts.

Sapphira's gentle voice broke in on her reflections. "I must say, Karenza, this description shows a most ravishing evening gown which would look quite delightful on dear Cressy. However, I cannot understand how the writer can one minute extol its virtue of being excessively economical and then, if you please, go on to say that the bodice is of green silk fastened with emeralds and diamonds! 'Pon my word, they have the oddest notions of economy."

"Indeed, my love, we shall have to resign ourselves to being positive dowds for the Season if such adornments become all the rage, for I fear that apparel of that nature is now well beyond our means," her twin declared in melancholy tones, determinedly ignoring the fact that her father's income had never provided them with sufficient funds to do more than dress in a very modest fashion.

"Nonsense! When we have our own seminary we shall soon be plump in the pocket and be able to command all the elegancies of life that we desire," Cressidia's declared optimistically. "And Jonathan says he will act as riding master for our pupils, for he has not—I am glad to say—forgotten his horsemanship. Indeed, I declare he will be an excellent instructor." There was more than just a glow of admiration for his equestrian abilities in her eyes as Cressidia spoke of her protégé.

Karenza drew in her breath sharply. "Jonathan! I had forgotten about him. Lud! I hope he will keep out of sight for the present. I feel I should have insisted on his removal to the village before our cousin's arrival."

"What! And leave him exposed to another attack by his unknown assailant. Oh no, Karenza, it would be a monstrous thing to do!"

"But Cressy dear, it is nearly a week since his accident, and there has been no sign of this mysterious enemy of whom you speak," her sister answered in a slightly exasperated tone. Before Cressidia could argue the matter any further, there came from without the windows the sound of clattering hooves on the carriageway and a subdued noise of bustle in the hall.

An uneasy silence fell upon the little group. Miss Brinton calmly replaced her knitting in her bag, while Miss Denny endeavoured to shrink even further into the background. A little self-consciously, Sapphira lay aside her journal and rose to move gracefully to her twin's side, taking Karenza's cold hand into her own and giving it a sympathetic squeeze. No words were necessary between them; each knew what the other was thinking and feeling.

A murmur of voices from the entrance hall indicated that the butler was greeting his new master; other members of the household staff were no doubt also making their bows and curtsies. Then the great double doors of the saloon were thrown open. "My Lord Darnborough and Mr Mapping," Datchett announced in sepulchre tones.

Slowly, Karenza rose to greet them, surprised and a little annoyed that the viscount should seek to thrust another stranger in their midst on such a delicate occasion. Obviously he was a man with little sensibility!

The viscount had already discarded his drab coat with its many capes into the waiting arms of the footman and came quietly forward, a slight smile on his lips and a curious glint in the grey eyes. Behind him Justin followed a little shyly.

As Karenza looked towards him, a half-stifled exclamation broke from her lips. She stood rooted to the spot, staring in outraged astonishment at the gentleman who had so rudely accosted her the previous day. One, moreover, who had the temerity to falsely endow himself with the name of Mr Marcus! How dare he deceive her so!

Sapphira shot an uneasy glance at her sister, aware of her unnaturally rigid stance and perplexed by her lack of greeting for the strangers in their midst.

His lordship, giving no indication of having already met one of his cousins, came across the room, hesitating momentarily in front of the twins before a swift glance at Karenza's flushed countenance enabled him to accurately identify his eldest ward.

"Miss Coningsby, I believe. I trust I have not kept you waiting." When she did not answer, being incapable of speech, merely staring at him with unbelieving eyes, the corners of his mouth twitched slightly. He ushered forward his young companion. "Pray, allow me to introduce another of your cousins and my nephew, Justin Mapping." Then as Justin made his bow to Karenza, his lordship, with practised ease, bestowed one of his most charming smiles on her twin. "And you must be Miss Sapphira. I am delighted to have the pleasure of making your acquaintance."

Sapphira hastily murmured conventional words of greeting, more concerned with her sister's unnatural behaviour. Conscious of the curious eyes upon her, Karenza forced herself to greet the young Mr Mapping and to assure him that she was only too delighted to make his acquaintance. Within moments she was in sufficient command of herself to introduce his lordship to his younger wards as well as their chaperones.

As she watched the viscount move amongst them, Karenza felt a rising tide of wrathful resentment. That the abominable and outrageous, albeit fascinating, Mr Marcus should be none other than their guardian, the sixth Viscount Darnborough, appalled and infuriated her. How he must have laughed to himself ever since the incident in the woods, no doubt imagining her embarrassment when they next met and probably joking about it with his nephew. Yes, and only someone totally devoid of all sensibilities would have brought along an unexpected guest on such a delicate occasion, and without so much as an enquiry as to whether it would be convenient or not for the family to receive him. But, of course, he no doubt felt it to be totally unnecessary to inform her of his intentions. He was, after all, the master of Darnborough Hall and could invite whom he liked whenever he wished. How arrogant and unfeeling of him to act in such a high-handed manner. Her thoughts fueled her fury, and she eyed him with active dislike as the viscount, after exchanging a few commonplaces with Miss Denny and leaving her positively overcome by such condescension, returned to her side.

"Can it really be true that you are indeed the sixth viscount?" Her voice was vibrant with a mixture of outrage and anger.

His amused glance raked her face. "I regret to say that I am."

"Regret? Oh, come now, you must think me the veriest greenhorn to believe one regrets such an inheritance!" Disbelief and dislike patterned her countenance.

"I always say what I mean, Miss Coningsby. I had no desire to succeed to your father's estate and all the responsibilities it entails."

She flushed at the implications behind his words. "There is nothing I could dislike more than for my sisters and me to be your wards! Since the feeling is obviously mutual, it will no doubt be easy to arrange that we meet but rarely."

"You have misunderstood my words, Miss Coningsby. There was nothing personal concerning yourself or your sisters in my desire not to succeed your father. However, the deed is done and the fact remains that you are all my wards. I have no intention of failing to accept my responsibilities and will carry out my duties as my conscience demands."

Her lips curled scornfully at these words. "It is useless for you to waste your eloquence upon me, sir. Such desire to fulfill your duties would perhaps have had some influence on us if you had shown the slightest inclination to fulfill them at the time of our greatest need, when papa died, instead of indulging in mere amusements for six months before condescending to claim your inheritance. However, I am happy to be able to inform you that my sisters and I will be withdrawing to our own quarters once you are in residence, where I trust we shall be spared the attentions of an obviously unrepentant rake!"

Lord Darnborough stiffened and a stern frown gave his face a forbidding look. Green eyes darting fiery sparks met icy grey ones. "I suggest, Miss Coningsby, that we agree to consider your comment unsaid." His tone was frostily polite. Karenza blushed furiously, extremely vexed with herself for having permitted her quick temper to exercise her tongue with such unruly words.

"I beg your pardon," she forced herself to say through stiff lips. He bowed and, apparently having no more to say to her, moved aside to make way for Justin, who having been chatting for some time with Sapphira now came up to her with an engaging smile on his face.

"I trust, ma'am, that I do not incommode you with my presence, but indeed I was so enchanted to learn that I had acquired so many delightful new relatives that I could not resist accompanying my uncle."

"The pleasure is ours, Mr Mapping," Karenza said kindly before adding in a more thoughtful tone, "Your mother is his lordship's younger sister, no doubt?" There was a startled gasp from Justin.

"Oh no, ma'am, she is his senior by several years."

"Really! You do surprise me. Why you look like father and son together." Then smiling brightly into the stunned face of the viscount, she added in artificially gracious tones, "I do assure you, Mr Manning, that your presence is more than welcome among us today. Indeed, there is no need for you to feel under any obligation to us at all, since we ourselves are but guests in what is now your uncle's residence."

"Oh surely not!" Justin protested, discomforted by the undertone of bitterness in her words.

"Miss Coningsby does me an injustice," Lord Darnborough suavely interrupted. "At no time could I nor would I consider the daughters of the late viscount as being any

other than, how shall I say, equal partners in this residence."
There was an unexpected note of warmth and sincerity in
his voice which took his listeners by surprise.

"Why, that's most kindly said, my lord." Sapphira raised
soft, appreciative eyes to his.

"Believe me, I do mean it," he assured them. "And pray,
since we are related, perhaps you could address me as
cousin."

"Not Mr Marcus?" Karenza said sotto voce, so that only
he could hear.

A dancing gleam of laughter came into the grey eyes
and the forbidding visage relaxed as he looked down at her.
"Oh, I don't think that is necessary, you little vixen, though
my first name is Marcus." For some reason the knowledge
that he had not completely deceived her comforted Karenza
and caused her to adopt a more conciliatory tone.

"Then, cousin, may I suggest you permit Datchett to
show you to your rooms, for we keep country hours and
dine at six-thirty. It would be unwise to upset cook, who
is no doubt impatiently waiting to lay before you her finest
dishes."

Karenza's forecast proved true, as dinner that evening
bore witness. Anxious that she should not lose her position
in the household to some fancy French chef, as was the
wont with many of the nobility, cook had excelled herself in
preparing a dinner fit for a king. Karenza, who had thought
she would be unable to partake of even the smallest morsel,
found the presence of Lord Darnborough and Cousin Justin
positively stimulating. Naturally she confined her conversation to Justin on her right and Cressidia on her left, while
Lord Darnborough's natural good breeding permitted him
no more than a slightly pensive stare at the overpowering
presence of the epergne in the table centre. With the merest
tremor of the voice, he began discussing its artistic merits

with Miss Brinton and Sapphira. Indeed, it was Karenza who soon found its presence an irritant, for she was no longer so averse to gazing upon his lordship's countenance at the far end of the table.

It was a pity that this period of goodwill was to be, alas, relatively short-lived. After the ladies withdrew on the arrival of Datchett with the port, Lord Darnborough lounged back in his chair and listened to the enthusiastic outpourings of his nephew.

"She has the looks of an angel, a voice as soft as a cooing dove and the sweetest smile I have ever seen, do you not agree, Marcus?" Justin spoke almost reverently.

"Are you referring to Karenza?"

"Oh no. At least I don't think so. 'Pon my soul, though, they are devilishly alike, but I think Sapphira has a more gentle look to her." Justin's eyes sparkled. "I can't tell you how pleased I am to have accompanied you here. I would not have missed it for anything!"

Lord Darnborough raised his brows in polite incredulity. "I am positively overwhelmed by your delight for my company, or is it perhaps that of Miss Sapphira Coningsby which inspires such enthusiasm?"

Justin gave a good-natured chuckle. "What a complete hand you are, Marcus. But tell me, do you not think that she is the most divine girl you have ever met?"

His uncle did not immediately reply. He sat looking enigmatically at his nephew for some moments, then picked up his quizzing glass to examine him with a meditative stare. Apparently satisfied by his scrutiny of the younger man, he lowered his quizzing glass and reached for his port before saying in a somewhat satirical tone, "Forgive me, but I find this change of heart a trifle overwhelming. If I mistake not, according to your passionate outpourings throughout much of our journey, your whole life would be blighted if consent was not given for your marriage to a certain young person out of a gaming house. Do I detect a change of heart?"

"Well, I think I perhaps mistook my feelings," Justin interposed airily, dismissing his earlier protestations of undying love with an apologetic shrug of his shoulders. "You know how it is," he said confidingly. "Maria's a lovely girl, but now, when I compare her with Sapphira, I see that she lacks that certain something; I don't know what it is."

"Quality," suggested his lordship, frowning somewhat absentmindedly into his glass as he twirled it round in his fingers, watching the light from the candles catching the edges of the crystal and causing a sparkle, which, for some reason, reminded him of the flashing eyes of his eldest ward.

"Yes, that's it!" enjoined his nephew enthusiastically. "She has a special quality and cousin Karenza, too," he added generously. "Don't you think they are both incredibly beautiful girls?" His voice brooked no argument, nor could the viscount disagree with him.

"Oh undoubtedly diamonds of the first water," his lordship commented a little wryly, well aware that he was unusually attracted by the lovely Karenza and finding his feelings a trifle disconcerting.

Justin continued his eulogy to his new ladylove. "Sapphira has such a kind and gentle disposition, and she is without the slightest pretence or guile."

Lord Darnborough shot his nephew an uneasy glance. He was well aware that his sister would scarcely thank him for rescuing her beloved son from the toils of one female only to have him fall in love with another, whose birth and breeding were indubitably superior to the unlamented Maria, but whose lack of fortune was to be deplored.

Unambitious for herself, Lady Manning nevertheless harboured the desire for a brilliant marriage for her elder son.

He was handsome, wealthy and moved in the best circles, yet remained a modest, pleasant youth who was totally impervious to his mother's efforts to provide him with a suitable wife. Yet, it was not just his sister's feelings that caused the viscount to seek to discourage Justin's tendre for his newly met cousin. The very circumstances under which they had met placed him in an awkward position. It would not be right for Lord Darnborough to encourage a girl who was his ward to commit herself to his nephew while she was still in mourning, and before she had seen anything of the world. It was better to quash the affair now, before either became seriously involved.

"What do you think of Sapphira, Marcus?" Justin's curiously shy tone broke in on his reverie.

"My dear Justin, when you have been on the town a little longer, you will be more up to the trickeries of the female mind, especially one out to capture a rich husband."

"Good God!" Justin exclaimed indignantly. "Surely you do not think of Cousin Sapphira as a designing creature out to trap me into marriage. I swear such a thought has never even entered her mind."

Meeting Justin's startled and outraged gaze, his lordship threw caution to the wind. Unaware that his words could be clearly overheard by Karenza, who had returned to the drawing room after a swift visit to console the disgruntled Misses Arabella and Drusilla, upset that they should have to partake of their supper apart from their elders, he continued to speak in a devastatingly distinct voice.

"I grant you that both Sapphira and Karenza are remarkably good-looking girls, but I can inform you, as one who has been unmercifully hunted by the female sex almost as soon as my elder brother breathed his last, that there is little to which they will not stoop in their desperation to entrap an eligible gentleman into matrimony. I have had them faint in my arms, after carefully observing that I was close to hand, sigh, weep and tell the most touching little tales of undying love. Unfortunately for them, I was also fully aware that had I been the ugliest and most unpleasant creature imaginable, their words of devotion would have remained unaltered, for only the loss of one's fortune would have cooled their ardour."

"Why, Marcus, you surely cannot place your own wards in such a category! I cannot accept that there is anything to support such allegations. They are the two kindest, most honest and open-hearted young ladies I have ever met." There was astonishment as well as indignation in the young man's tone.

"But then you have not met as many women in your life as I have," said Darnborough coolly.

"Well, no. I suppose I haven't, but I still think your words to be monstrously unjust. It is not their fault they have no fortune. It is indeed an intolerable position for them to be practically dependent on the goodwill of strangers."

"Which is exactly why they would wish to find themselves rich husbands."

"Do you also consider Karenza to have designs on me?"

"No, I fancy that I may be her target!" his lordship rejoined equitably.

Justin looked troubled. "I do not understand how you can regard your wards so badly, for they have done naught to earn such contempt."

Lord Darnborough rose to his feet and stretched his long limbs. "Wait until you are better acquainted with the female sex before condemning me. Now I suggest we join the ladies."

"I am surprised you do not wish to retire immediately," Justin said stiffly.

"Now, what could have given you that impression?" said his lordship, moving to the fireplace and jerking the bellpull beside it.

Justin stood up, still puzzled by his uncle's attitude. "Anyway, I still think you are wrong about our cousins."

"Possibly, but not likely," replied his relative with cool certainty.

"You rang, my lord?" Datchett's voice brought an abrupt end to the conversation.

His lordship turned his head. "Yes, I rang. Pray, conduct us to the drawing room. Come, Justin, we will rejoin the ladies."

6

H is lordship might have appeared less composed had he been aware that the advice he had tendered his nephew was now ringing in the ears of a furiously indignant Karenza.

At first scarcely able to believe that the new Lord Darnborough was referring to Sapphira and herself, Karenza had stood dumbfounded on the bottom stair, near the partly opened door of the dining room. But as the words penetrated her mind, she grasped the banisters tightly, as though to restrain herself from marching in and giving his lordship a tongue lashing that would remain with him for the rest of his life.

How dare he, she fumed, shaking with anger. How dare he insinuate that she and dear, sweet Sapphira were seeking to entrap them in matrimony. What arrogance! What conceit! Why, her lovely sister had only to make her appearance on the London scene to become the most desirable female and future wife to men of far greater standing than young Mr Mapping!

Karenza's wave of anger was immediately followed by a most unusual desire to weep. For a moment she had thought that she had found a real friend, someone with whom she could speak frankly and with whom she could share laughter. Instead, he considered her no more than a designing hussy, with her eyes fixed only on his fortune. If only she had been a man and could challenge him to a duel to pay for such an insult!

As the viscount rang the bell to summon Datchett, Karenza forced herself to move swiftly towards the drawing room. Overcome by disappointment and anger, she felt unable to face the rest of the evening in the company of the now detestable and contemptible Lord Darnborough. No sooner had she entered the drawing room than she announced she had a headache and would retire to her chamber immediately, at the same time charging Miss Brinton to make her apologies to the gentlemen. Brushing off the chorus of concerned voices at her statement, Karenza firmly indicated that she desired to be left strictly alone, for she would soon be better if left undisturbed.

One look at her twin's stormy face with its flashing green eyes had been enough to warn Sapphira that now was not the time to ply Karenza with questions. Her sister's words were taken with no further demur than a gentle suggestion that she had indeed suffered a most strenuous day and she, Sapphira, was quite sure that Lord Darnborough and Mr Mapping would understand dear Karenza's need to retire early. Sending her sister a grateful glance, Karenza departed, anxious to be gone before the two men made their appearance.

It was some time before Karenza could finally rid herself of the fussing attentions of old nurse, who was convinced that her lambkin was in need of her expertise and was all for bringing her a variety of hot possets, at the same time scolding her for overexerting herself that day. But at last she was alone, able to sink back on her pillows and recall once more those hateful and hurtful words uttered by the viscount. What should she do now, she wondered.

How could she show her guardian how false were his assumptions concerning Sapphira and herself and teach him a much needed lesson in humility, too? Never had she felt so insulted, and revenge for such a humiliation was certainly demanded.

One plan after another flitted through her mind. For a brief moment, a picture of Sir James challenging his lordship to a duel—pistols for two and breakfast for one—crossed her mind, but almost immediately she rejected the idea, wryly admitting to herself that it was more likely it would be Sir James's body stretched out on the grass rather than his lordship's. Besides, she had the melancholy conviction that Sir James would not wish to fight a duel on her behalf; in fact, he would probably consider it rather vulgar!

The solution, when it came, brought an unexpected smile to Karenza's lips as her mind probed and tested its strengths and weaknesses. Finally she was convinced. Yes, she had found a way to achieve total independence of the sixth viscount for all the family. She would show him how totally unfounded were his allegations that she and Sapphira were on the lookout for rich husbands, and once her object was achieved, she would have nothing further to do with him. He would be cut right out of her life forever! Almost purring with contentment, Karenza finally drifted off into a deep sleep which even the heavy rainstorm that night failed to disturb. Could she have but known, she would need all her energies to put her plan into action.

Karenza did not appear at the breakfast table the next morning, and Lord Darnborough was conscious of a feeling of near disappointment as his eyes, scanning the lovely faces of his wards, noted her absence. Justin; already adapting to the early hours and simple life style of his cousins, was engaged in trying to coax Sapphira to ride with him that morning, while Cressidia was softly urging Miss Brinton to accompany her to visit Jonathan as soon as it was convenient.

Miss Brinton, however, had other things on her mind, for Karenza had confided to her, as well as Sapphira, all that Lord Darnborough had said the previous evening. She had been shocked and dismayed by his lordship's calumny, and on his polite enquiry on the health of his eldest ward, she had answered him in her most terse tones, stating that Karenza had already breakfasted, not being one to lie abed in the morning.

Noting the admonitory tone of her voice, the viscount shot a surprised look at the elderly lady. Before he could speak further, however, Justin was laughingly protesting that he was prepared to rise with the sun if only Cousin Sapphira would promise to do likewise and allow him to escort her for a morning ride while the rest of the world was abed.

Before any reply could be made, Karenza's cool tones cut in on the conversation as she entered by the open French windows. "I regret that we lack suitable mounts for you to ride, cousin, unless you have brought your own horses, for, unhappily, I have had to dispose of most of my father's animals."

A swift frown darkened his lordship's brow as he rose to greet her. "Surely that was not necessary, so soon after your father's death," he said bluntly.

Karenza sketched him a swift curtsey before answering him. "Pray, forgive me, sir, for reminding you of the fact that it is over six months since our sad loss and we had many pressing needs." She paused before adding with devastating directness, "Since we had no one to turn to, it was the only way to solve some of our more immediate problems."

A dull flush came to his lordship's face, and he cast her a sideways look, his eyes curiously regretful. "It appears that I owe you an apology for my apparent tardiness, but I had no idea that—"

She did not allow him to complete his sentence. shrugging her shoulders impatiently as she cut him short. "It is of no importance now, my lord. We look not to you for financial support. We have our own home and an income, small though it might be, which will ensure that we do not become your pensioners."

"That is not a matter I care to discuss at the breakfast table," the viscount said blightingly. "However, I wish to make quite clear that as your guardian, I shall maintain you all as befits members of my family, and on that point you can rest assured. As for your father's stable, I regret that you have disposed of the horses, but I shall replace them."

"If you wish to establish your own stable here, that is entirely up to you," Karenza stated calmly. "But my father's string was left to me and did not form part of the estate. I could not afford to keep them all and did not, anyway, consider them suitable for your purposes. My father was a bruising rider and his horses required handling by a first-rate horseman. No doubt you can hire a more docile creature from the inn in the village to use until you leave," she added with a look of bland innocence.

There was a startled gasp from Justin at her words before he sprang to his uncle's defence. "Oh no, Cousin Karenza, I promise you that Marcus is a first-class rider. Why, he hunts regularly with the Quorn and the Pytchley, no mean feat, I assure you."

Karenza appeared unimpressed by these words. "No doubt that is why he had to be rescued from the ditch where his horse deposited him but yesterday," she said disparagingly.

A chuckle broke from Justin's lips as he cast a look at his lordship standing with an unfathomable expression on his face.

"I wonder how," said his lordship, his eyes narrowed, "you should come to know of my unfortunate mishap, cousin?"

Thrown into some confusion, she answered stammeringly, "Well, of course, the servants mentioned it, having heard the story, no doubt, from one who had visited the inn."

"Oh, pray, what happened?" Sapphira and Cressidia spoke in chorus.

"Shall you tell the story, Karenza, or shall I?" Looking up, she saw his grey eyes gleaming with mockery and could not doubt that he was enjoying her discomfiture. A feeling of resentment rose within her that he should be so wholly devoid of chivalry. Accurately reading the expression that flitted across her face, his lordship gave a humorous shrug of his shoulders as he spoke. "You will indeed think me the rawest of greenhorns, but as I rode through some woods yesterday morning, a curst mongrel attacked my horse, which promptly deposited me amidst some brambles, due no doubt to my attention being distracted by the sight of its owner. I can only plead that I was totally unprepared for the onslaught—my own fault, of course!"

There was an outburst of shocked little cries at such misfortune, whereupon a puzzled frown crossed Justin's face. "But why should you have been distracted by the owner?"

His lordship glanced at him sardonically. "Can you not guess?"

"Oh, a beautiful maiden appeared, I suppose," Justin said laughingly.

"An apparition of loveliness," enjoined his lordship cordially. "Indeed, I fancy her to have been something quite out of the ordinary, but a real termagant, alas! I shudder even now when I think of the expressions she used in the presence of a gentleman." He ignored Karenza's stifled gasp. "Such a setdown I received," he added mournfully.

"A very unfortunate occurrence," said Miss Brinton calmly, not at all sure that she approved of the turn the conversation had taken.

"It must have been Maggie Baker, the blacksmith's eldest daughter," Sapphira's quietly interposed. "Don't you think so, Karenza?"

Recovering from her stupefaction at his words, Karenza stiffly owned that it was most likely the case, then hastily diverted their attention by informing the viscount that the bailiff awaited him, at his convenience. Datchett would show him to the estate office when he was ready to meet with the man, unless he would prefer Mr Morden to come to the library.

With laughter still lurking in the corner of his eyes, his lordship solemnly thanked her for so kindly arranging the matter before adding, "I should be grateful for your company at this meeting, Karenza, for I have a lot to learn, and I gather that you have an excellent understanding of all estate matters."

For a moment Karenza was taken back, not only by the compliment that he paid her, but also by the sincerity of his tone. Then memories of his words of the previous evening came flooding back, and she was determined to show him very clearly that she was not interested in earning his regard, or of ingratiating herself with him in any way at all. She answered him coolly. "I am sure you do Mr Morden an injustice, cousin. He is well acquainted with all the details concerning the estate and would no doubt enjoy the honour of discussing its matters with you. I have more important things to attend to."

If his lordship was disconcerted by these words or the frigid tones in which they were uttered, he showed no sign of it, merely fixing her with a speculative gaze as he repeated her words. "More important matters to attend to? Come, come, Karenza, you shock me. What can be more important than the welfare of the people whose livelihood depends upon Darnborough Hall and its lands?" he asked with mocking reproachfulness.

Cold green eyes met quizzical grey ones as Karenza paused to choose her words carefully. "They are all your responsibility now, cousin," she said emphatically. "They are no longer any concern of myself or my sisters. As I have just said, our energies must now be directed to our own future and the many problems it undoubtedly contains for us. However, those are matters in which, despite your earlier declarations of responsibility for us, I shall seek neither your involvement nor your assistance, you may rest assured of that."

There was a silence as the little group around the table absorbed her harsh words. Justin looked troubled, but was given no opportunity to speak as his lordship addressed his eldest ward. "Pray, explain yourself further, Karenza," he demanded affably. "Do I detect a repudiation of myself as guardian of the Misses Coningsby? If so, I fear you have misjudged me. I am not one to refuse the demands made on me by your late father or to tolerate any willful denial of my right to carry out my obligations as your guardian." He cast an amused glance at the slim figure standing so stiffly before him, a stray beam of morning sunlight setting the red hair aglow. "Come now, let us be friends," he added coaxingly. "I promise you that I am not the monster you appear to make me out."

Karenza appeared unmoved by his words. "Let me put the matter more plainly," she said icily. "As I have already said, we have a very small income, but however small it may be, we shall never come to you for financial assistance. As for being our legal guardian, I accept that as a regrettable fact, but since Sapphira and I come of age in six months, it is something which we at least shall not have to suffer for long. In the meantime, I intend to investigate ways in which we can supplement our finances through our own efforts. Since we have our own accommodation, what we do there is our concern alone."

There were startled gasps from her sisters and Miss Brinton at her outspokenness. "Oh, Karenza, my love, you really should not speak thus of such matters," Miss Brinton was moved to say, appalled by her young relative's forceful words in front of them all.

Justin, unable to endure the thought that the beautiful Sapphira should have to suffer so much as a moment's discomfort over her future, was moved to say protestingly, "But cousin Karenza, there can be no need for any action by you to further your fortunes, for Marcus would be only too happy to care for you all, is that not so, Marcus?" Thus appealed to, his lordship inclined his head to signify his assent to these words while gazing very thoughtfully at the disdainful look on the face of the young lady before him.

"There, I told you so!" Justin exclaimed triumphantly. "Besides, I daresay it will not be long before you are married," he added ingenuously. Then recalling the recent loss of their father, he blushed furiously and stammered out, "I mean, of course, after you are out of mourning. Do, pray, forgive my words if they have offended you." He looked appealingly at Sapphira, who found herself automatically responding to him.

"Of course we do, dear sir. We know your thoughts were kindly meant." Then she blushed at the warm look in his eyes as they rested gratefully on her lovely face.

"I see no reason for the ladies to reject my concern for their well-being. It is only to be expected that I should make provision for those members of my family who are also my wards." His lordship's languid tone appeared to dismiss Karenza's remarks as being of little importance.

Karenza glared at him before saying fiercely, her voice vibrant with loathing, "Under no circumstances would we accept your charity."

He raised an eyebrow at the vehemence of her words. "And how, may I ask, do you intend to finance yourselves?" he enquired, eyeing his fulminating ward with an amused but not entirely unsympathetic look.

"It is of little concern to you, sir," she snapped.

"Oh, but it is," he answered her gently. "Your father and the law have invested me with the responsibility for the care of you and your sisters."

"Well, in six months time Sapphira and I can do as we wish within the confines of our own part of the house," she said defiantly. Miss Brinton moved uneasily in her chair, recognizing in his lordship a man whose pride would never permit the fruition of Karenza's plan for independence.

"I think you will find there are certain limitations to your freedom of action," the viscount murmured thoughtfully, "but do enlighten me further, unless of course you fear what I might say."

"Afraid of what you might say!" Karenza gasped, bridling with indignation. "I have no fear of you."

"I rather thought as much," his lordship commented dryly.

Karenza eyed him with dislike. "Well, if you must know, one of my plans is to set up a seminary for young ladies in the west wing."

"A very select one," interposed Cressidia, adding hopefully, "and of course the fees will be extremely high so only the best of the ton could afford to attend."

The viscount appeared strangely unmoved by their words. "I'm afraid I cannot permit it," he said in an apologetic tone.

Karenza's eyes widened in shock. "I do not require your permission," she said bluntly. "You cannot prevent me doing as I wish."

"Oh, but I can," Lord Darnborough replied amiably.

Sapphira gave a puzzled frown as she glanced up at him. "But how could you do so?" she asked in a gentle voice. "It is, after all, our home, and we do not include the main building in our scheme of things. Surely we can do as we wish there."

A sardonic smile lingered upon their guardian's lips. "Legally speaking, you are quite right. But lord, I shall enjoy seeing the look on the fond mamas' faces as they arrive with their beloved daughters to be met by the interested stares and ogling of half the rakes in London."

"You would not dare!" breathed Karenza, shocked by his outrageous suggestion.

"Oh, but I would. Justin will confirm that I do not kindly tolerate opposition to my wishes."

"Would you really invite a lot of wild young men to Darnborough Hall?" Cressidia sounded more intrigued than shocked by this prospect.

The viscount gave a grim little smile. "If I considered it necessary, I would most certainly do so. However, I trust that your sister's natural good sense will prevail and spare us all such an unseemly occurrence." The faint touch of hauteur in his voice brought an angry flush to Karenza's face as she addressed him.

"We will not be beholdened to you; the idea is anathema to us all. I—"

"Don't be so commonplace, Karenza, it doesn't become you. You are my wards and my responsibility. Accept the situation. Oh, don't look so aghast, dear cousin! Am I so abominable that you cannot believe my desire to assist you is genuine?"

His last few words surprised her, and for a moment she suspected him of mockery, but the sardonic look was gone from his eyes. Karenza was temporarily disconcerted. She had an almost overwhelming desire to believe him and allow him to shoulder the burdens that were becoming so heavy for her to carry. Yet, there was no way she could ignore what he had said the previous evening, speaking when he had no idea of her proximity. Surely those words represented his true feelings, whatever he might now say. No! She was not to be taken in by a few kind words, merely uttered to soothe her feelings once his lordship had gained his victory over her.

Karenza regarded him frostily. "I wish you would rid yourself of the notion that you are essential to our well-being. I regret if I sound churlish and ungrateful, but I can only reiterate our lack of desire to be the recipients of your charity."

Lord Darnborough said nothing, compressing his lips as though endeavouring to keep back some acid retort, while a frown creased his brow.

Karenza paused, watching the effect of her words before adding bitingly, "I accept that you can prevent the use of our home as a seminary, but there are other ways by which we can provide for ourselves." Then casting her adversary a darkling look, she swept from the room without another word, glad that she had spent the previous night in contemplation of an even more scandalous plan.

There was a painful silence after she left. Sapphira hastened to break it by rising to her feet, saying in a soft voice as she did so, "I fear Mr Morden will be wondering what has become of you, sir. Would you wish me to accompany you to meet him?" She looked enquiringly at her guardian, wondering as she did so why Karenza should be so opposed to accepting the generous help offered by this handsome and elegant man. It was a pity, to be sure, that his unfortunate words last night should have been overheard by her sister, but gentlemen often said things they did not really mean, and she could not but feel that his offer to care for them was a genuine one. If only he had been more tactful with Karenza and not sought so obviously to impose his will on her. Karenza would never accept his domination, she knew, not ever.

Immersed in her thoughts, Sapphira did not hear his lordship's answer until Cressidia's impatient voice broke in, "Oh, for goodness sake, Sapphira, do take Cousin Darnborough to the estate office, for there is so much to be done today." Sapphira looked up to see his lordship regarding her with such an understanding expression on his face, it was almost as if he could read her thoughts, but his words were quite unexceptional. "I am ready when you are, cousin." He bowed and opened the door for her, ignoring her confused apologies for allowing her attention to wander.

As they went through the door, Justin called out to her, "Pray do not be too long, cousin, for if we cannot ride together, you could perhaps show me your charming garden." Sapphira turned to give her smiling assent, but Miss Brinton, feeling it was high time she made her presence felt, reminded her young relative of her promise to accompany her two youngest sisters and herself to visit their dear friend Clara, who had suffered the misfortune of a broken ankle, thus leaving Justin with nothing more to do than beg the privilege of escorting the ladies on their short journey later that morning.

7

Karenza, making the most of her momentary freedom, had sent the footman to request Jonathan's presence in the west wing, where she hoped to have the opportunity to put to him the plan she had hatched the previous night.

No sooner had the young man been ushered in by a somewhat scandalised Datchett, than Karenza, disregarding the normal courtesies, eyed him speculatively before saying bluntly, "Jonathan, tell me, how sure are you of your skills as a horseman? Please be honest in your assessment of your capabilities; it is of the utmost importance for me to know."

He looked at her in astonishment, for she seemed unusually serious, but he answered her readily enough. "I seem to have a natural affinity with horses." He paused, then seeing the uncertain look on her face, smiled encouragingly at her. "My wits might have gone abegging as far as my name and background are concerned, yet I am oddly certain of possessing a high degree of competence insofar as the handling of such animals are involved. But come, tell me why you are so anxious to learn of my skills, Karenza?" He spoke to her with the easy familiarity of one of the family, for, as he had rather sadly pointed out, he knew them better than anyone else, and they, in turn, were happy to extend to him the comfort of being regarded more as a brother than a guest. Except of course for Cressidia, whose regard for the handsome young man was of a much warmer, personal nature.

Karenza carefully avoided answering his question as she took several anxious paces about the room before coming back to stand in front of him, looking with an almost painful intensity into his eyes. "Could you train a horse for a race? By that I mean get it used to racing procedures as well as instructing its rider in the finer points of racing techniques?" The note of urgency in her voice caused Jonathan to regard her a little uneasily before he answered.

"Well, I think so." He frowned.

"What's the matter?" she asked sharply.

"Flat racing or over fences?"

"Oh, on the flat. It is a race concerned purely with speed." Then in a burst of confidence she added, "Sir Peter Sharples of Buckley Manor has offered a purse of five thousand guineas to the owner of any horse that can beat his favourite, Ulysses. Just imagine, five thousand guineas! And I have the only animal that stands a chance of winning, Buccaneer!"

There was no doubt that Jonathan's interest was kindled by her words. His eyes took on a faraway look as he pondered the challenge presented to him, and he began mentally assessing the difficulties he would need to surmount if he took on the task his benefactress so urgently required of him. "You would need a good jockey. Unfortunately, I weigh almost twelve and a half stone, and that is too great a weight for Buccaneer to carry if the race is of any considerable length. What is its distance?"

Karenza thought for a moment. "I believe it is quite a long race, something over three miles, twenty-five, maybe twenty-six furlongs. But the distance would suit Buccaneer; he needs time to develop his speed, he is not a sprinter."

"And the rider? He is a strong animal, but at the same time the lighter the weight he carries, the easier it will be for him."

She hesitated a moment before answering him, uncertain of what his reaction would be. Still, Karenza realised that she had little choice, Jonathan could not be kept in ignorance for long. Taking a deep breath, she gazed up into into his enquiring brown eyes. "I shall ride him myself."

"You!" There was no doubting the shocked incredulity in his voice.

She gave a wry smile. "I have known Buccaneer since he was born and have ridden him often. Indeed, I am one of the few people who can ride him; we have a very good understanding of each other."

"But you're a girl!" Jonathan's horrified reaction made Karenza realise more than ever that what she planned was against all rules of propriety and would place her beyond the pale of Society if her escapade became known. As to the manner in which her guardian would receive the news, that needed little imagination. At the thought of the viscount, her lips tightened and she faced the young man determined that no one should prevent the fruition of her plan.

"I daresay my idea may seem a trifle unusual to you. But to win that race would give my sisters and me our independence. If I ask too much of you, then I can but apologise and will not make any further demands on your time." The note of sad reproach in her voice was not lost on her companion, who gave an exasperated sigh before saying somewhat bitterly, "You know very well that I cannot deny you your request, for I am too deeply obliged to you to do so, but I still think it's a crazy idea and one which could ruin rather than save your future."

Wisely, Karenza chose to ignore his last few words, instead thanking him with warm effusiveness for his kindly act in coming to their rescue. Then wasting no further time on unnecessary pleasantries, she was soon in deep discussion over the practicalities of her scheme and plans for preparing Buccaneer for his great race.

On further questioning by Jonathan, Karenza revealed that Sir Peter, who was inordinately proud of his racing stable, was seeking to enliven the approaching end of the flat racing season with a private race on his own estate. It would also have the advantage of amusing his guests, amongst whom, it was rumoured, would appear one of the royal dukes. Such an entertainment, which would be greatly to their liking, would at the same time enable Sir Peter to indulge in his favourite pastime of exhibiting the extraordinary prowess of his favourite animal, Ulysses. The race was scheduled to take place at the end of the month, thus there was no time to lose.

Before Jonathan could voice any further doubts on the matter, the door opened and Cressidia came hurrying in, looking a trifle flustered. "Oh, there you are, Jonathan! I have been looking for you everywhere." She paused and glanced uncertainly at Karenza as Jonathan swept her a bow and raised her fingers to his lips. "Datchett told me you were here, too, Karenza, so I knew you would not object if I joined you."

Before Karenza could disabuse her mind of this assumption, Jonathan spoke in a humorously wry tone. "My dear Miss Cressidia, I am always more than happy to see you at any time, but this morning your presence is more than welcome. Pray, help me to rid my mind of a dreadful fear that has assailed it."

"Dreadful fear? You? Why, what do you mean?" She looked up at him in wide-eyed astonishment at his words.

He gazed down at her. "Tell me, my dear girl, does insanity run in your family?"

"How dare you, sir, make such an infamous suggestion!" Cressidia blazed forth, scarcely able to believe her ears.

He ignored her protest, while Karenza showed every sign of succumbing to a fit of giggles. "Because your beloved elder sister has just suggested that I should train Buccaneer for her to ride in a five-thousand-guinea race at Buckle Manor, at which most of the county would be present, including no doubt your guardian."

"Oh, what a brilliant idea! She would win, of course! Oh, my darling, clever sister." Cressidia gave a little crow of delight. "How exciting."

Jonathan gave a heavy sigh. "Can't you see that such an act, even if Karenza won the race, could mean your social ruin? Society would never condone such behaviour, all of you would be ostracised by every member of the ton. As for your guardian, he would no doubt consign the whole lot of you to bedlam, and few would blame him!"

"Well, I must say, I never thought you would be the one to preach propriety." Cressidia sounded disgusted at her hero's lack of spirit.

"I have no intention of being discovered," Karenza said firmly. "I shall appear just before the race starts, suitably disguised of course, and disappear immediately after it. Jonathan can also place bets on our behalf, like papa did, so that we shall win much more than just the prize money."

Jonathan clutched his head between his hands and, casting his eyes heavenwards, gave a groan of despair. "What, in God's name, ma'am, gives you the idea that you are bound to win this race? Believe me, you could lose everything, including your good name and that of your sisters, too," he added reproachfully.

Avoiding his eyes, Karenza responded with a lightness she was far from feeling. "I know this sounds to you the maddest of beliefs, but I promise you, Jonathan, that I am certain I shall win. I, too, have no desire to become a social outcast, and, indeed, I intend that none will ever know of my action." Her lips tightened and her chin jutted out as she added tersely, "I am absolutely determined to go ahead with my plan; it is the only solution to our problems."

Cressidia, knowing her sister when she spoke thus would brook no more argument, hastened to prevent her love from trying her sister's patience further, saying placatingly, "Well, if anyone can train Buccaneer, it will be Jonathan." Then she smiled angelically at her suitor.

Jonathan gave a short bark of laughter before saying in a still far from mollified tone, "I simply cannot understand why Karenza refuses to accept financial support from Lord Darnborough. He is now head of the family, and his offer as you described it to me, Cressidia, seems quite unexceptional."

Karenza hesitated before telling him her reasons. She felt peculiarly reluctant to expose the less pleasant side of his lordship's character to their scorn and disapprobation. Then, choosing her words carefully, she explained some of what she had overheard that fateful evening, reducing as much as possible the conceit and arrogance portrayed by the viscount. Even so, her hearers were warm in their condemnation of Darnborough, and Jonathan, his eyes fiery with indignation, vowed that nothing would prevent him for doing exactly as his lovely benefactress required of him.

Relieved that she would encounter no further argument, Karenza bestowed a warm smile on her two companions before adding hopefully, "I daresay he will be gone within a few days, for our cousin will, no doubt, find our simple way of life very flat after all he is used to doing."

"Well, I trust you are right," Jonathan remarked bluntly, "for he would be the oddest of guardians not to object most violently to your proposed action, and I have my own special reasons for not wishing to make him my enemy." He looked meaningfully at Cressidia, who blushed a rosy red and appeared adorably confused.

A swift frown crossed Karenza's face. Much of her ambition was centred on providing for her younger sister all the advantages of a coming-out Season, which had been denied the twins. She also considered Cressidia far too young to form, as yet, any serious attachment, especially to this young stranger, who, though the most delightful of companions, suffered from the overwhelming disadvantage of not knowing who he was or from whence he came. It was certainly not a situation to which she could give any encouragement, regardless of her present need for Jonathan's assistance. Then giving her head a shake, as though to dismiss her unwelcome thoughts, Karenza politely enquired of her sister whether or not she would be accompanying Miss Brinton and Sapphira to see her good friend Clara, who was perhaps expecting her arrival in the near future.

Cressidia gave a gasp of dismay. "Oh dear, I had quite forgotten the arrangement, but perhaps I could excuse myself, Sapphira and Drusilla will not mind." She glanced wistfully at Jonathan as she spoke, who beamed his approval at her suggestion. But their pleasure was short-lived.

"I daresay you would wish to remain at home, Cressy, but since Clara Seymour is one of your closest friends, I think it would be shameful to treat her so, especially as she has risen but recently from her sickbed. I know her mama is most anxious to allay her spirits, which are sadly depressed at the moment." Karenza's reproachful tone brought such a look of guilt to Cressidia's face that her sister had to bite her lip to stop herself laughing.

"Oh, dear me, no of course I would not wish to disappoint Clara, except that Jonathan will . . . I mean that he may . . . wish for me to try to assist him to recover his memory by um . . . er . . ." Here Cressidia sought wildly for an excuse which would merit her neglect of one who had been her closest confidante since childhood.

Karenza interrupted her, saying coolly, "There is no need to deny Clara the pleasure of your company, Cressy, as I hope that Jonathan will allow me the pleasure of his company in establishing Buccaneer's training programme this afternoon. It is a matter that will take some time. Indeed, it is a most opportune moment for us to visit the stables, since Cousin Darnborough will no doubt be accompanying Mr Morden for the rest of the day. They have much to see and discuss. That is, of course, if you are agreeable, Jonathan." Not missing the minatory note in her voice, Jonathan bowed his assent, at the same time casting a surreptitious wink at Cressidia.

"Indeed, Cressy," he said with a whimsical smile, "you must not deny me the opportunity to repay, in part at least, the many kindnesses I have received from your family. Miss Karenza is right; there is much to be done, and therefore I shall bid you adieu." Giving her no time to object, he sketched a bow to both ladies before retreating to the door, where he proceeded to spoil the elegance of his exit by poking his head around the door post in a stealthy manner, demanding of a passing footman if the coast was clear of his lordship and his nephew, and on receiving a reply in the affirmative he departed, pausing only to throw over his shoulder a last word to Karenza in an exaggerated whisper. "Psst! I shall hide myself in the stable with Buccaneer. Pray, look very closely at the third bale of hay on the right; it will mark my abode." Then with a cheeky grin and a last wave of his hand he was gone, leaving both girls gazing after him, struggling to contain their mirth.

While Karenza and Cressidia were thus engaged, Justin seized his chance to waylay the lovely Sapphira as she came lightly down the stairs, having donned an enchanting bonnet of chip straw which was tied most becomingly with a green satin ribbon that matched her eyes.

Much moved by this apparition of loveliness, Justin offered her his arm as she descended from the last step, and with almost unconscious reverence found himself softly quoting in a tender tone as he looked down on her

> "If I could write the beauty of your eyes
> And in fresh numbers number all your graces,
> The age to come would say, 'This poet lies;
> Such heavenly touches ne'er touch'd earthly faces.' "

The hand resting on his coated arm trembled slightly, and a blush suffused her lovely visage as Sapphira raised glowing eyes to meet Justin's worshipful gaze. For a moment neither spoke, then Sapphira said with gentle wonder, "You are a poet, sir, and do me great honour."

"Alas, I cannot claim the words for my own, but pray that you will accept that Shakespeare is but expressing, most aptly, the feelings in my heart!" There was no mistaking the sincerity of his words, and as if to seal a secret bond between them, Justin raised her hand to his lips and bestowed on it a reverential kiss.

"I am quite overcome by your compliments," Sapphira said, a trifle breathlessly. "I feel sure we should not be speaking thus, but I confess," she added with quiet dignity, "that I am more than a little touched by the warmth of your regard." In her heart she was convinced that Justin was undoubtedly one of the handsomest, cleverest and most wonderful young men she was ever likely to meet.

What more they might have said to each other was abruptly terminated by the appearance of Datchett with news that the carriage was at the door and Miss Brinton would be grateful if Miss Sapphira and Miss Cressidia would join her immediately. With a tremulous smile in his direction, Sapphira moved obediently towards the front doorway, leaving Justin gazing after her, reluctant to let her pass from his sight and bewildered by the unusual depth of his feelings for his beautiful cousin.

 8

No sooner had Karenza sought to retrace her steps in search of her shawl before departing to the stables than the portly figure of the butler appeared, wearing a slightly harassed expression.

"Well, what is it now, Datchett?" She was impatient to be gone before Lord Darnborough returned to the Hall.

"It's Sir James, Miss Karenza." Correctly interpreting the look of exasperation on her face, he added apologetically, "I was unable to say you were not at home, ma'am, because he had met Miss Brinton whilst she and Miss Sapphira were waiting outside in the carriage for Miss Cressidia, and she mentioned that you were here." He paused before adding with a darkling look, "And there is another gentleman with him, too, a Mr Faversham." The expressionless tone of his voice immediately informed Karenza that their dignified and elderly retainer did not approve of Sir James's companion.

A puzzled frown crossed her forehead. "Mr Faversham? Surely you mean Sir Henry Faversham? Though I recall hearing that he has taken to his bed and is very ill." Karenza thought for a moment of the old man who resided but five miles from her home and who had been a friend of her grandfather.

Datchett's voice broke in on her musings. "It's not Sir

Henry, Miss Karenza, but Mr Percy, one of his grandsons. I believe that in some circles he is known as Beau Faversham." His tone indicated his disapproval of the owner of this appendation.

Karenza regarded him enquiringly. "Beau Faversham?" she repeated, sounding a trifle bewildered.

"That's right, miss." Then seeing her continuing puzzlement, he went on to recount to her, with ill-concealed gusto, the scandalous doings of the Faversham family, rumours of which she vaguely recalled hearing as a child. "Sir Henry had two sons, Miss Karenza. There was the elder one, Mr Sylvester, who upped and eloped with some nabob's daughter. Sir Henry refused to have anything to do with him after that, or so it is said, but it's common knowledge that the marriage was a happy one. They had one child, a boy, not that Sir Henry would ever see him, though he was his heir after Mr Sylvester died in some foreign place, India I think it was. Then there was the younger son, Mr Basil, a bad lot he turned out to be! He married well but gambled away every penny of his fortune before getting killed in some duel over a game of cards; someone accused him of cheating, or so I've heard tell. It's his son, Mr Percy, or Beau Faversham as he likes to be known, who's here now. I can't think why, for it is said, and I've no doubt it's true, that Sir Henry doesn't much like him either—'a fish-faced tailor's dummy' is what Sir Henry called him the last time he visited his grandfather." Datchett spoke these words with relish, as one not often given the opportunity to speak thus of his betters.

Karenza had long ago ceased to be amazed at the amount of personal detail concerning the local gentry that was common knowledge to the villagers, and Datchett had always been one to keep his ear to the ground. He beamed down on her now, a fatherly figure, pleased to be able to give his young mistress all the details, which a nicely brought up young lady could not rightly ask for.

She managed to restrict her smile to a slight twitch of the lips. "That will be all; thank you, Datchett." She spoke with cool dignity which was totally lost on one who not only had known her since babyhood, but who had, moreover, bestowed many a sugarplum or some other comfit on occasions when she had occurred parental wrath and was banished to her room with no more sustenance than meagre fare of bread and milk until she should see the error of her ways.

"Now, don't you bother your pretty little head about Mr Faversham, Miss Karenza," he said comfortingly, "because I've already sent a respectful request to Miss Denny to receive him and Sir James in the blue salon, not that she's the sort of lady to be able to hold much of a conversation with such gentlemen!" He gave a derisory sniff, having his own opinion of the place a governess should hold in a nobleman's establishment.

"Well, perhaps he has called to see Lord Darnborough," said Karenza hopefully, giving up her halfhearted efforts to put a stop to Datchett's flow of gossip and kindly concern for her.

"I don't think so, miss. Neither he nor Sir James mentioned his lordship. Do you wish me to ascertain Lord Darnborough's whereabouts and request his presence on your behalf?"

"Certainly not! Come, Datchett, you must not be so prejudiced. I am sure that Mr Faversham is a quite unexceptional young man."

Yet, as Karenza entered the salon where a flustered Miss Denny was making somewhat laboured conversation with their visitors, it was all she could do not to gasp in amazement at the spectacle presented for her gratification. Her words of greeting died on her lips as she gazed, with some stupefaction, upon the exquisite young dandy who came mincing up to her as she stood in the doorway.

He was of average height, slightly built and with a pale complexion. His features were delicately moulded, almost at variance with the hard, calculating brown eyes which surveyed her with surprising coldness. Nothing could have been more exquisite, however, than the careful arrangement of his hair, brushed upward into a feathery quiff, or the cut of his double-breasted coat, claret coloured, with sage-green kerseymere breeches. Following the dictates of the ultrafashionable, his neck was enveloped by a cravat arranged in a style known as the Mathematical to the initiated. His shirt collar rose so high as to make his head appear immovable, and from one delicate hand dangled a highly scented handkerchief, while the other held an elaborately wrought quizzing glass that hung on a gold chain around his neck.

"Ah, Miss Coningsby," he said in a soft, lisping voice as he bowed over her hand with incomparable grace. "I am honoured to have this opportunity to renew our acquaintanceship."

Karenza bestowed on him a cool smile as she sketched him a graceful curtsey. "It is always a pleasure to welcome to Darnborough Hall a member of Sir Henry's family, Mr Faversham," she replied civilly, "though I fear, sir, that I cannot recall any previous meeting between ourselves."

"Indeed, ma'am, it was not to be expected that you should remember the occasion when our respective grandfathers introduced us. You were, so I believe, a mere infant of five years to my nine; yet, such an impression you made on me that I have never forgotten that event."

Karenza could only hope that her countenance did not betray her total disbelief in his utterances as she responded lightly saying, " 'Pon my word, sir, I can but wonder at your remarkable memory."

"Yes, it is quite incredible, is it not?" He preened himself, taking what she said as an expression of admiration for his mental prowess. "But, pray, permit me to offer you my belated but undoubtedly sincere condolences on the unhappy demise of your dear father. Being in this part of the country in order to bestow on my grandfather the pleasure of my presence, I felt impelled to call and offer you my deepest sympathy. I am quite put out of countenance by the fact that I should have been so remiss as to absent myself from his obsequies, but I was, alas, unavoidably detained in town. Ah! poor Lord Darnborough! Such a memorable character. I am sure you must greatly miss him."

"You are most kind, Mr Faversham. I did not realise that you were a friend of my father." Karenza faltered, quite dazed by this flow of eloquence.

"Alas, ma'am, I can claim to be no more than his admirer," he replied. "Your father was one for whom I have always had the very highest regard, and when by chance I came across my good friend Sir James, and learnt that he was en route for Darnborough Hall, it seemed a propitious moment to express my feeling to you personally, Miss Coningsby. Dear me, I am quite overcome to think of the sad loss to this little community of one of its leading figures."

Karenza scarcely knew what to say, for the dictates of civility forbade her giving utterance to her real thoughts concerning this young man's protestations.

Sir James, who had been standing unusually silent until that moment, felt the need to assert his claim as Karenza's protector as well as to disabuse the Beau of his illusion of friendship between them. A soul of convention himself, he held members of the dandy set in abhorrence and was still confused as to the manner in which the Beau had persuaded him to accept his company on encountering him in the village less than an hour ago. He spoke more bluntly than was his wont.

"You informed us that you were on your way to visit Sir Henry. I am sure Miss Coningsby will not wish to delay you further, for we are aware of your grandfather's ill-health, and no doubt you are anxious to see how he goes." The note of distaste in his voice was all too apparent, and Karenza, enjoying one of those rare moments of feeling positively in charity with her suitor, gladly came to his support.

"Oh, pray, do not allow us to detain you at such a time. I would not wish to give Sir Henry cause for disquiet, since he must be awaiting your arrival with impatience," she prevaricated, deeply conscious of Datchett's words to her on Sir Henry's feelings for his younger grandson.

Beau Faversham answered them with unshaken urbanity. "I do not wish to put you to any inconvenience, Miss Coningsby, but as you know, it is a considerable time since Sir Henry has had the honour of being a guest in this house, yet he still refers to your beautiful gardens. It would perhaps cheer him to hear that I had visited them. Would it incommode you greatly if I took a gentle per-ambulation before my departure? Pray, tell me if I ask too much of you.

Reluctantly, Karenza felt obliged to disclaim any such feeling and to say that she would be happy to accompany him. With a swift look at Sir James, she included him in the expedition.

Since it was already late summer, the garden was no longer looking its best, and this, coupled to the Beau's obvi-ous lack of horticultural knowledge, increased Karenza's sense of unease, which rapidly heightened to alarm when she noted that the Beau's perambulations were taking them slowly, but surely, in the direction of the stables.

"I feel certain, Mr Faversham," she proclaimed with a bright smile, "that Sir Henry would delight in learning of your opinion of the Lime Walk. The trees look particularly magnificent at this time of the year and—"

He interrupted her with an affected little cry. "Oh, ma'am, I wonder if I might beg a brief visit to the stables, since I see they are so near. For you are to be felicitated on your possession of that paragon of equine virtue, the great black stallion that your dear father once informed Sir Henry was destined to become the greatest racehorse of this century. I yearn to see him with my own eyes—pray, do not deny me such a pleasure!" As Karenza frantically cast about in her mind for some excuse, he cast her an uncomfortably penetrating look before adding smoothly, "My grandfather would benefit more from hearing my description of that great creature, I believe he is called Buccaneer, is he not, than from all the medications at present thrust upon him. Do not, ma'am, I beg of you, deprive him of such joy."

Beside him, Sir James gave a disbelieving snort, seemingly unimpressed by the Beau's filial beliefs and annoyed that he should have to share Karenza's company any longer. "Surely Sir Henry's interest in such matters would be less than his desire to see his grandson, when time may be of importance to one in such a frail state," he said with marked asperity.

The Beau gave an exaggerated sigh. "Alas, I fear that my grandsire's passion for the turf and its adherents outweighs all other considerations. He would undoubtedly prefer an account of the great Buccaneer than the filial presence of one who cannot aspire to membership of the FHC let alone be accounted a bruising rider like the late viscount."

Completely unimpressed by this self-abnegation, Karenza was about to challenge his assertions when her eye was caught by Lord Darnborough strolling casually in front of the stables with the dastardly Homer at his heels. She drew in her breath sharply at the sight and mentally castigated herself for directing Jonathan to meet her at the stables when his lordship obviously had not the slightest qualm about intruding upon the Misses Coningsbys' private property. She had to draw his attention away from Jonathan's hiding place at all costs. Disregarding her immediate aversion to Beau Faversham's request, she surprised her companions with the speed with which she now urged them along the pathway, saying chattily as she did so, "I see my cousin is near us and would no doubt be pleased to make your acquaintanceship. You must know, Mr Faversham, that Lord Darnborough has only recently come amongst us and is but now making his first tour of the estate." She stopped short of informing them that this tour did not include the part they were nearing. She would have words with his lordship about that aspect later.

The Beau inclined his head. "Indeed, ma'am, you are to be felicitated on achieving the status of being the wards of such a nonpareil." There was an almost sneering note to his words which caused her to shoot him a look of surprise.

"You are a friend of Lord Darnborough?" she enquired, struggling to hide her aversion to the situation he had described.

"We are known to each other." The words were unrevealing, yet Karenza received the impression that he bore no great liking for the new viscount.

With a slight jolt, Karenza realised that his lordship was standing in close proximity to Buccaneer's stable as he awaited their arrival. As they came up to him, the viscount bowed slightly in Karenza's direction. Then holding up his quizzing glass, he surveyed the Beau's appearance, eyeing him deliberately from top to toe, taking in the slightly muddied boots before saying with exaggerated astonishment, "My dear Percy, what a surprise to see you here! Pray, tell me to what do I owe the honour of this visit?"

The Beau trod delicately across the muddied ground towards the viscount, a hand held out and smiling. "Ah, you see before you a devoted grandson en route to present his filial respects to a worthy grandsire, but desirous of first paying his respects to the family of an old acquaintance. And how are you, my good Marcus? Allow me to offer you my sincerest congratulations upon your new inheritance."

"Thank you." His lordship's tone was dry. "I am quite overcome that you should suffer an interruption to your journey to call on us."

The Beau shuddered. "Pray, do not remind me of the hardships of my travel. I swear that every bone in my body has been shaken by the roughness of these roads." As he spoke, Karenza noticed that his eyes moved restlessly, seldom staying long on any one spot. She was convinced that he was looking for something—or could it be someone? Anxious to divert attention from Buccaneer's stable, she saw with relief that Sir James, still hovering uncertainly on the outskirts of the little group, was regarding his beloved in an anticipatory manner.

"Oh, do forgive me, James!" Having claimed their attention with her words, she turned to her guardian, meeting his speculative stare with all the nonchalance she could summon to her aid. "Allow me to present a good neighbour and friend of the family, Sir James Ledbury. James, this is Lord Darnborough."

They looked each other over in silent appraisal, then Lord Darnborough moved forward. "It is a pleasure to meet a friend of my young charges. How do you do." He gave a charming smile as he spoke and extended his hand.

Though visibly gratified by the warmth of his greeting,

Sir James, still anxious to establish what he considered to be his special relationship with the Coningsbys, responded with polite but restrained civility. "Your lordship is quite right in saying I am a friend of the family, but I consider myself more than just a friend to one of them." And here his eyes rested meaningfully on Karenza's suddenly flushed face. She opened her mouth to give him a sharp setdown for his presumption, but aware of the amused gaze of her guardian, who had correctly interpreted her look of annoyance, decided to deny him the pleasure of having his omnipotence confirmed by her.

Unaware that during this interchange Beau Faversham had drawn nearer to Buccaneer's stable, she was suddenly startled by a wild neighing sound and the crash of hooves against the stable door. Much alarmed, the little group swung round in time to see the Beau backing hastily away from the big black stallion, whose ears were laid back close to his head, his eyes rolling wickedly as he gave forth another angry scream and reared up in his box.

Frightened that Buccaneer might harm himself, Karenza shot towards her beloved stallion, calling soothingly to him as she went.

"What a damnable brute! He should be put down!" It was the Beau who spoke, his usually languid tones now heightened by a mixture of shock and fear.

Karenza swung round at these words, her eyes flashing in anger as she came to the defence of her precious Buccaneer. "You had no right to approach his stable thus. What did you do to frighten him so?" she asked, regarding the dandified figure with fierce dislike.

"I did nothing, I assure you," the Beau protested. "All I did was to go to look at him. I laid not a finger on the creature; there was certainly no cause for such a reaction. I vow he is a vicious monster," he ended indignantly.

"He is not vicious," Karenza snapped furiously. "He must simply have realised that you were afraid of him and resented your fear." Her lip curled scornfully as she spoke.

The Beau eyed her with ill-concealed dislike. "I cannot felicitate you on your perspicacity, ma'am, since what you say is not true. I swear that it was nothing on my part which caused this animal to act thus."

His lordship, feeling the need to calm the situation, interrupted the pair. "Pray, allow me to take this opportunity to invite you, my dear Percy, to partake of some refreshment. I have an excellent brandy, which will assist in soothing your shattered nerves."

As Karenza turned to open the stable door, a question from the Beau caused her to freeze in her tracks.

"Have you heard about the wounded highwayman in this area, Marcus? It is believed that he could be hidden somewhere on your estate."

Karenza could only be thankful that her back was towards the men as he spoke. Even so, she could not restrain a gasp of horror as the implications of his words sunk in, and for a moment her calm deserted her. Jonathan a highwayman! Oh no, it could not be so! It would break Cressy's heart. Deeply shocked, she turned to face her tormentor, keeping her face expressionless as she addressed him. " 'Pon my soul, sir, do you try to frighten us by such remarks? There are no highwaymen in our part of the world. Come, you must be indulging your imagination."

There was an odd expression in his eyes, hard to interpret, yet somewhat disquietening, as he answered her. "Indeed, ma'am," the Beau said coldly, "I assure you that I had the story not a few hours ago when partaking of some refreshment at the village inn. A tale of a wounded man being found in your own woods—wounded, no doubt, when escaping from the scene of his crime."

Good God! How had he come to hear of them finding Jonathan? One of the servants must have been unable to restrain his tongue and let slip—when in his cups, no doubt—the story of their finding the young, wounded gentleman. Karenza had to discover the extent of the Beau's knowledge, and more importantly, why he was so concerned with this event, for she was ready to swear there was an avidity to his interest that contrasted sharply with his apparent role as a mere recipient of local tittle-tattle.

The cool tones of her guardian broke in on her troubled thoughts. He seemed to have an uncanny awareness of the questions she wanted answered but was too afraid to ask.

"Come, come, my dear Percy, you see me all ears. Pray, enlighten my ignorance concerning this mysterious event, for I swear I have no knowledge of such happenings, yet was myself a guest at the inn but a day or so ago."

The Beau hesitated, as though uncertain of how to reply to these words. Then he emitted a high-pitched little laugh before shrugging his shoulders in a nonchalant manner and saying, "Well, I daresay I may have been misled, but I was informed, quite earnestly by some ancient denizen of the village, that there had been an attempted holdup, not far from where we are now, and in the ensuing melee, one of the gang—a youngish, brown-haired ruffian—had been fired upon and wounded, yet not so badly that he was unable to make his escape. There was some rumour that he had been found and hidden in a local abode. No doubt he is a handsome fellow, whose dark, flashing eyes could cause some female's heart to melt—you know how women are in such matters." He gave a knowing snigger before delicately placing a pinch of snuff on the back of his hand and inhaling it, his gaze resting speculatively on Karenza's stony countenance.

She threw him a withering look of contempt, but before she could give tongue to her dislike of his insinuations, Sir James unexpectedly entered the fray, frowning slightly as he did so. " 'Pon my soul, sir, I have heard naught of such an occurrence," he said ponderously. "Such a happening would be of general knowledge within a matter of hours in a close-knit community such as ours, and certainly as a local magistrate, I would undoubtedly have been informed of the crime. No, no, sir. I fear your informant was indulging in a little rustic humour at your expense. Sadly disrespectful, no doubt, but then one must make allowances . . ." though the little chuckle Sir James gave indicated his personal enjoyment of the jest played upon the dandy.

The Beau shot him an annoyed glance before turning to Lord Darnborough, who had listened to the exchange with an ill-concealed air of boredom. "I would be glad to accept your kindly offer of a brandy, Marcus." He sounded pettish to Karenza's ears. "I vow I still suffer from the shock of that great brute's attack on me. My advice to you is to have it shot before it kills someone."

"No one has any authority to do anything to Buccaneer, sir, for he is mine and mine alone!" Karenza's words burst hotly from her lips, but it was at her cousin that she looked, challenging him to argue the matter.

Darnborough made no comment, but he gave a slightly ironical bow to her before turning to the Beau and saying, with a touch of impatience in his voice, "Well, we had best make our way to the house, for you will no doubt not wish to render Sir Henry anxious by your continued absence." Then he paused, before adding with devastating directness, "Will Sir Henry's other grandson be joining you at his bedside? I've heard that Sylvester's son has returned from India."

The Beau's face seemed to pale as shock held him rigid.

His eyes were frozen pebbles as he echoed the viscount's words. "Sylvester's son?" He made a palpable effort to regain his equilibrium. "I don't know what you mean."

"Come, come, man, your cousin, your uncle's only child." Lord Darnborough's tone was affable, but there was an inscrutable look in his eyes as he pressed on with the subject. "I heard that Sir Henry was at last anxious to meet his other surviving grandson. I suppose the fact that the boy is his heir has influenced his decision, at least that is what I heard but a week or so ago."

The Beau gave a ghastly smile. "You have the advantage of me on the subject, Marcus, for I swear that I know nothing of my cousin's possible arrival. It is probably no more than some idle speculation."

"Indeed!" replied Darnborough, politely incredulous. "I would have thought the source of my information to be highly reliable."

"Oh, who was it? I wonder if I know him." The Beau spoke casually, but his voice was strained and his hand shook slightly as he sought to inhale some more snuff, while Karenza and Sir James remained silent but fascinated onlookers.

The viscount looked the Beau over meditatively before answering him. "I daresay you are acquainted with her," he said gently, "for it was none other than Sir Henry's younger sister, your aunt, Lady Wainforth. She was quite excited at the prospect of meeting her great-nephew."

"Aunt Sarah!" Beau Faversham's voice betrayed the shock this news had given him. "I vow I had no knowledge myself of the impending visit of my dear cousin. What a pleasant surprise you have bestowed on me, Marcus." The quick words were belied by the coldly murderous look on his face as he spoke. Then turning abruptly on his heel, Beau Faversham strode off in the direction of the house, rudely disregarding his host, who gazed thoughtfully after him before turning to Sir James to urge him to accompany them both and bidding Karenza to join them as soon as she was free to do so.

 9

Karenza stared after the retreating figures in a sombre mood before returning to Buccaneer's stable and slipping quietly inside. The horse moved a little restlessly as she peered anxiously through the gloom of the interior. "Jonathan, are you there?" she hissed, keeping her voice low in case one of the grooms should hear her. Although those still remaining had been sworn to secrecy, she was not sure that one of them had not already divulged news of their unexpected guest, or so the Beau's comments seemed to indicate.

There was a movement in the heap of hay below the feeding trough, and Jonathan, festooned with many of its pieces, emerged from his hiding place, sneezing heartily as he did so. " 'Pon my soul, I thought all was lost when your friend seemed about to enter the stable." Jonathan started to brush the hay vigorously out of his hair and clothes, his brown eyes twinkling with laughter as he gazed down at Karenza as she coaxed Buccaneer away from his corner.

"He is no friend of mine," she retorted indignantly. "What a dreadful creature he is, with his dandified clothes and lisping voice—and he was frightened of Buccaneer!" Then she frowned slightly. "I must confess that I was surprised at Buccaneer rearing and kicking out in such a fashion."

"It was my fault, I'm afraid," Jonathan said slightly apologetically. "I jabbed him a bit suddenly in the rump with a stick to make him act up and deter the entry of your visitor. I'm sorry to give this magnificent creature such a fright, but it was all I could think of on the spur of the moment."

Karenza cast an anxious eye over the animal's gleaming hindquarters and ran a gentle hand across them, relieved to see no flinching or other indication of a tender spot. "Well, he seems to have suffered no harm, and he certainly gave that odious little mushroom a veritable fright, for which I am extremely glad." Then she recalled the Beau's accusations and turned a concerned face in Jonathan's direction.

"There is something I must tell you." She hesitated a moment before continuing, trying to choose her words carefully, not wanting to offend the young man on whom she now depended for so much, yet determined, above all, to protect her darling Cressy from an attachment to one who could possibly end up on the gallows. "Mr Faversham made mention of an attempted holdup by a highwayman or of his escape after being wounded and he—"

"And you think it could be me?" He interrupted her in tones of strong indignation, looking at Karenza with an expression of shock mixed with hurt on his face.

She was strongly desirous of immediately assuring him she thought nothing of the kind, but resisted the temptation and answered him firmly. "I daresay it is no more than the prattle of a malicious tongue, but"—here Karenza regarded him with anxious eyes—"can you be sure you were not involved in any way if you have no memory of the occasion?"

"I must portray a remarkably devious character if you consider that it is even possible for me to be no more than a common criminal. I don't need to regain my memory to be quite certain that I am innocent of such a charge. I am astonished, ma'am, that you should be willing to accept the veriest suggestion that such could be the case, especially emanating from one, whom I can only describe as being a smoke-faced, ramshackle court card!" There was no sign of guilt in the open, young face before her, only wrathful amazement at her question.

"Oh, pray do not fly into a great fuzz," she begged him. "I do not for one moment believe any ill of you, but tell me, why should Mr Faversham recount such a falsehood, and why should he be so anxious to find you? For I swear that was the purpose of his visit."

"I can give you no reasons for Mr Faversham's accusations, though I can see that it may be difficult for you to accept my protestations of innocence of the charges he has leveled against me." Jonathan answered her stiffly, still mortified by her doubts of him. "I will relieve you of the embarrassment of my presence, ma'am."

"Don't you dare abandon us!" Karenza said sharply.

"But I cannot prove that I'm no criminal, any more than I can prove that I have no idea why Mr Faversham has impugned my character thus, so how can you wish me to remain with you and your sisters?" By now the poor young man was in a state of total bewilderment.

"Oh don't be so caper-witted, Jonathan," she pleaded. "We need you here quite as much as you need us until you have regained your memory. As for Mr Faversham's assertions, I think it was but a canterbury tale to account for his own mysterious interests in your whereabouts."

"Why should you be so certain that is the case?" he remarked with asperity.

"Because Sir James said that such a crime would have to be reported to him. He's the local magistrate, you know, and very conscious of his duties, I assure you. He stated that no word had come to his ears of such happenings. I do not know why I did not remember that sooner—my wits must have gone abegging—pray, forgive me." She cast him a charming smile. "Now I must hasten to the Hall, or my cousin will be seeking me to see why I have not returned. I'm afraid you will have to remain in hiding a little longer, but I will, I vow, be back as soon as is possible. Do not, I beg of you, attempt yet to return to the house—there are so many persons about." She moved out of the stable door as she spoke.

Jonathan gave a groan mixed with another bout of sneezing. "Egad, I'm ready for a jar and am wishful of saying good-bye to my present quarters, yet I'll do as you request of me and keep company with my good friend here." With this, he gave the nudging head of the big horse a friendly pat, and picking up a handful of straw, began to brush down the black satin coat, hissing lightly between his teeth as he did so. Karenza gave a final friendly wave of her hand and departed, trying to devise en route some explanation to account for her extended absence.

She found Lord Darnborough with her would-be suitor in the drawing room and paused on the threshold, an expression of contrition crossing her face at the sight of the viscount stoically enduring an undoubtedly tedious account of Sir James's visit to Mr Cokes's experimental farm in Norfolk. With no more than the slightest lightening in the grey eyes did his lordship indicate any pleasure at this interruption to Sir James's soliloquy. He rose to greet her, saying as he did so, "Well, Karenza, I fear that one of your guests was unable to await your return and bade me to make his excuses to you. Sir James, however, was kind enough to keep me company."

She shot him a suspicious look, but the blandly smiling face gave little away as she crossed the room. Ignoring him, Karenza put out her hand to Sir James. "I do beg your pardon. It was most remiss of me to have absented myself for so long, but Buccaneer was very restless, and it took me much time to soothe him."

Sir James looked grave and replied very earnestly, "I cannot but consider an animal of such size and uncertain temper to be totally unfit for a delicate female. I would wish, sir," he said, addressing his lordship, "that as Miss Coningsby's guardian, you could perhaps persuade her to be rid of the creature."

Forestalling Karenza's acid rejoinder, the viscount tactfully pointed out it was perhaps respect for a fond parent's prize possession that gave rise to Karenza's reluctance to part with him. Did not Sir James consider, perhaps, that such filial devotion was a most admirable trait in the young lady and should have their encouragement. Here his ungrateful ward gave a slight choking sound as she turned away to hide the laughter that threatened to overwhelm her at his lordship's unctuous tone, so at variance with the smile in his eyes.

Sir James said nothing for a moment as he absorbed these words. Then he gave an apologetic glance towards Karenza's back. "It is indeed as you say. I have been too concerned for Miss Coningsby's well-being, for which you must blame the natural inclinations of a devoted admirer. I shall say no more on that score now, but shall seek to address you further on the matter when the family is no longer in mourning."

A gleam entered his lordship's eyes as he absorbed the implications of these words, but before he could enquire further of Sir James's intentions, Karenza, with a faint flush on her cheeks and a decided edge to her voice, cut in. "Really, James, I wish you would rid yourself of such ill-conceived notions. My future will shortly lie in my own hands and will not require any consultation with his lordship or anyone else."

"Which is no doubt intended to put me nicely in my place," commented Lord Darnborough, looking singularly unperturbed by his ward's outburst, while Sir James went on to protest that she had, indeed, misunderstood him and that he did not intend to indicate that his lordship could bestow her hand on her suitor. Here he lost himself in a confused welter of words that continued until he finally took his leave, to the relief of both his host and hostess.

The viscount, interpreting with fiendish accuracy the expression on his ward's face as they watched Datchett escort Sir James out, said with mock severity, "I see, Karenza, that you have an alternative to your seminary at hand. Pray, inform me as to when I shall have the honour of leading you up the aisle."

Misunderstanding the mockery in his voice, Karenza turned on him sharply. "It so happens, sir," she stated in a quelling tone, "that I do not contemplate marriage with any gentleman of my acquaintance, and I find such mention of the subject by you excessively repugnant. I daresay," she added, determined to establish the fact beyond all doubt, "that I shall never marry!"

"Never?" repeated his lordship, appearing singularly unimpressed by the vehemence of her declaration.

"Never!" she repeated emphatically, raising her eyes to his, only to find him regarding her with a look of such amused disbelief that she was obliged to turn away, lest she should betray her own lack of conviction in her declaration.

Regaining her composure, she turned to face him once more. "What I wish to make quite clear to you, my lord, is that I do not look to matrimony to provide a solution to my difficulties. For though Society accepts such marriages of convenience, such a one would not suit me. I will marry only where my heart is involved, and that may never happen." Then, as a palpable afterthought, she added, "And Sapphira shares my views."

"In which case," said Lord Darnborough, opening his snuffbox with a practised hand and taking a delicate pinch, "there seems little likelihood of any nuptial celebrations at Darnborough Hall in the foreseeable future."

"Except your own, perhaps?"

"Mine!" His lordship looked momentarily startled.

"No doubt an arranged marriage to some wealthy and suitably well-bred heiress is what you have in mind for yourself," Karenza said in a sweetly innocent tone as her guardian regarded her through narrowing eyes. "Such an arrangement would be most suitable, since you, no doubt, scorn the more tender-hearted approach of us poor females. Pray, tell me, shall we soon be wishing you joy, cousin?"

"Wishing me joy!" he repeated, casting his ward a grim look. "Fortunately not, Karenza. Though your consideration of my character does me little credit, I am happy to inform you that I, too, neither seek nor wish for a complaisant spouse or a marriage where my affections are not engaged."

There was an unexpectedly stern note to his voice which surprised her, and she became aware of a sense of reserve in him at odds with his earlier friendliness. For a moment she almost regretted the impulse that had made her address him thus.

Seeking to find words to fill the silence that now hung awkwardly between them, Karenza moved uncertainly towards the window before saying with studied nonchalance, "Well, I am very glad to hear you speak thus, but you cannot expect me to associate such delicacy of mind with one who has not, so far as we are concerned, shown any appreciation of our feelings."

"If you are alluding to your desire to establish a seminary, then I will admit that your feelings were not foremost in my thoughts when expressing my opposition to the matter. However, if you are referring to my apparent tardiness in making my appearance at Darnborough Hall and assuming my duties there, then I can only express my very deep regret and most heartily wish that I had not failed you at such a time. Believe me, I would desire that you had no reason to think so badly of me."

His lordship's tone had now lost its accustomed coolness, and Karenza was surprisingly moved by the sincerity of his words, though feeling at a loss as how to reply to them. She could scarcely tell him that her deepest resentment of him sprung from having overheard the derogatory remarks he had made to his nephew on the subject of herself and her dearest Sapphira, the memory of which still rankled deeply.

A slight indication of her head and a gentle, "You are kind to say so, sir," hid the confusion of her thoughts as she sought to change the tenor of their conversation. It was with some relief that Karenza recalled the viscount's words to Beau Faversham concerning Sir Henry's elder grandson. She raised her eyes to where her guardian, propped against the mantelpiece, gazed meditatively down at her.

"I was most interested, cousin, in your talk of Sir Henry's heir. Can it be true that Sir Henry has requested his presence?"

"I believe so," responded his lordship dryly, apparently unaffected by the sudden change of conversation.

"Are you acquainted with the young man?" she asked, curious.

"I'm afraid not," said the viscount apologetically. "Do you wish me to become so? I am yours to command."

Karenza shot him a startled look, which he met with a bland smile. "Of course," added his lordship thoughtfully, "if his grandfather takes to him, he could inherit not only the title but also a considerable estate—a possibility which seems to engender a certain fear in our friend Beau Faversham if I mistake not."

"Do you really think that the Beau resents the very existence of his cousin?"

"I am quite certain he does. Do not be misled by Percy Faversham's foppish manner, my dear Karenza. He is no fool and not one to be easily crossed. If I were Sylvester's son, I would tread very carefully when in the vicinity of the Beau. For only he stands between Percy Faversham and the inheritance which the Beau, rightly or wrongly, feels should be his."

Silently Karenza absorbed his words, wondering if she had any justification for the vague suspicion that had just crossed her mind. "Do you know the name of Sylvester's son?" she asked slowly, inwardly debating whether or not this was the right moment to inform her guardian of Jonathan's existence and all that had befallen him. But before she could unburden herself, his lordship's next words fell knell-like on her ears.

"I fear, Karenza, that you may be concerning yourself overmuch with the Faversham family, or," he added, with a hint of laughter in his voice, "perhaps you are envisaging him as a suitable husband for one of your sisters. Such a match-making tendency in one so young quite overwhelms me!"

Misinterpreting the teasing note in his voice for one of mockery, Karenza cast him an icy look. "I do not appreciate such comments," she said in a forceful tone, abandoning any idea of informing his lordship of his unknown guest. "I am merely interested in the family's situation, since

whoever succeeds Sir Henry will become our neighbour."
Then feeling no desire to spend any further time in the
company of one who exhibited such a sad lack of respect
for the elder Miss Coningsby, Karenza swung round on
her heel and made her way to the door, declaring as she
paused with her hand on the door knob, "I am sure you
must be finding our quiet way of life excessively boring.
You must not," she added with a touch of irony, "permit
a misplaced sense of duty to keep you from your friends
and your normal social pleasures."

"You have no cause to denigrate yourself so, my dear
cousin. Whilst a certain touch of humility in a young lady
is to be recommended, it is not an attribute in which you
should over-indulge," his lordship rejoined caustically.

"I am not expressing any feelings of humility," she
snapped.

"You disappoint me." His lordship was unperturbed.

"All I wanted to ask was if, if . . ." Her voice trailed off
as she realised that she could not, in fact, demand of him
the knowledge she required.

"You want to ask when I shall be leaving Darnborough
Hall?" the viscount said obligingly. There was a good deal
of comprehension in his eyes, which were considering her
with an amused, rather than offended, gleam.

"Yes," she stated baldly, feeling little need to consider
the normal courtesies when dealing with one so obviously
devoid of all sensitivity.

"After Christmas," he said promptly.

"Christmas!" Karenza echoed, aghast. "You cannot be
serious!"

"Oh, but I am," he declared, wondering at himself as
he spoke, for it had been his intention to leave within
the sennight. "Do I detect a desire for my speedy departure?"

Karenza could not immediately answer him. What was she to do about Jonathan and training Buccaneer for his race? How like the viscount to be so inconsiderate, she thought bitterly. When needed, he did not come. Now when they were happily preparing for a life on their own, he not only had appeared on the scene, but had had the temerity to imply that he enjoyed their company, which anyone but a goosecap would know to be a shocking untruth. Well, she would not give him the satisfaction of putting her out of countenance, and as for commenting on her wish for his departure, she would not be so discourteous as to make her preference known.

"I am sure that as master of Darnborough Hall it is for you alone to decide when you come or go," she said dismissively and whisked herself from the room before her guardian could offer any further comment, leaving him gazing thoughtfully after her.

Gaining the solitude of her room in the west wing, Karenza paced up and down, her mind confused not only by her guardian's statement but also by the events of the afternoon, which had formulated yet another problem for her. Abandoning her ponderings on Lord Darnborough, she resolutely turned her mind to examining the odd coincidence of the assault on Jonathan and the appearance of Beau Faversham. Could there be a link between them? Was it remotely possible that Sir Henry's legal heir was none other than their nameless guest? She recalled the moment she had first gazed on Jonathan's unconscious face and the feeling that it was one that she knew. Was it of Sir Henry she was thinking, or someone else? Karenza frowned, trying to recall the old man's features, but it had been a long time since she had seen him, and he remained only a shadowy figure in her mind.

Sapphira's soft voice at her door broke in on her thoughts. With a sense of relief Karenza bade her enter. She listened patiently but with less than her usual concern to Sapphira's account of poor Clara's progress and Lady Sinclair's worries that she might not be well enough to face the rigours of her first Season. Finally, unable to contain her thoughts any longer, she began to recount to her twin the day's events in some detail, including her suspicions of Jonathan's identity and ending with the announcement, in sepulchre tones, of the viscount's decision to stay until Christmas.

"And Cousin Justin, too?" asked Sapphira with an unusually joyful note to her voice.

Karenza shot her twin an exasperated glance. "He did not say, but I expect that Lady Mapping will be anticipating her son's return in the near future."

Sapphira's face fell. "Oh yes, I suppose you are right, but I shall miss him," she added a little sadly.

Karenza gave an inward groan of despair. She needed her sister's wholehearted support in her undeclared war with their guardian, and she was not likely to get it if her twin fancied herself in love with young Mr Mapping.

"Never mind Cousin Justin," Karenza said sternly. "We have more important matters to consider. I must confess that I did not take Cressy seriously when she alleged that Jonathan could be in danger, but after today's visit by Beau Faversham, I feel that she may be right. We must think of a way in which we can discover whether or not he is Sir Henry's elder grandson—but without exposing his whereabouts."

Sapphira clasped her hands together in an agitated manner. "Surely he must have some member of his family who could identify him. There must be someone who is missing him and seeks to know what has happened to him."

"I fear that the only one who is seeking him is Beau Faversham, and my greatest concern is that he might find him here," Karenza answered grimly.

The two sisters looked at each other in silence before Sapphira made a tentative suggestion. "Could we not consult Cousin Darnborough?"

Karenza shook her head impatiently. "We should then have to account for hiding him here, and that is something I do not care to do. Besides, he has already suggested that my interest in Sir Henry's grandson is to entrap him in a marriage with one of my sisters!"

"What an odious thing to say!" Sapphira's tone reflected her sense of outrage.

"Yes," agreed her twin. "And what is more, just think of how Cressidia's warm feelings for Jonathan would strike his lordship. Oh dear, was there ever such a tangle!"

" 'Oh what a tangled web we weave, When first we practise to deceive,' " Sapphira quoted with a whimsical smile. "Never mind, my dearest, I'm sure we will come about in the end. You'll find a way, I know you will." She gave her sister a quick hug.

Touched by her twin's confidence in her abilities, Karenza gave an answering smile. "Well, perhaps something will occur to me later. In the meantime we must change, for we dine in but half an hour. I think that I shall make my excuses to retire early tonight. It has been an exhausting day."

"Cousin Darnborough will be disappointed," said Sapphira thoughtfully.

"Nonsense! I daresay he will enjoy the peace offered by my absence, for we argue whenever we are together," Karenza replied briskly, but her sister looked unconvinced.

10

Karenza's plan to slip quietly away after they had dined was thwarted by the persistent demands of the younger Misses Coningsbys to be allowed to join their elders when supper was over and the gentlemen had rejoined the ladies. The unexpected addition of his lordship's voice begging her to give them permission silenced the objections that rose to Karenza's lips.

Rather to her surprise, his lordship showed a positive enthusiasm for a game of speculation and an unexpected competence at jack straws, so it was a merry party that finally broke up for tea at nine o'clock. Miss Denny swept off two reluctant young ladies, who declared that they had spent the jolliest of evenings, and it was clear from their glances of approbation as Lord Darnborough bade them a friendly good night that they were finding their status as his wards less onerous than anticipated.

Any idea Karenza may have had of departing in their wake was once more defeated by the sight of Sapphira being led, gently protesting, to the pianoforte, where Mr Mapping persuaded her to render a perfect ending to a delightful evening by honouring them with one or two songs. With becoming reluctance, Sapphira seated herself at the instrument. Her admirer gallantly offered to turn the sheets of music for her while she played and sang.

Karenza shot an uneasy glance at his lordship and received from him only a sardonic look. However, she was pleased to see that as her twin finished her song, he joined in the applause and thanked her with every appearance of genuine pleasure, so that Karenza felt unusually amiable towards him and was prepared to greet him kindly as he moved across to her. She made room for him to sit down beside her and smilingly agreed that she, too, had enjoyed the evening. Indeed, had she not felt so anxious over her failure to meet Jonathan as promised, she would have regretted it ending.

She saw the viscount's eyes rest on his nephew, who stood happily chatting to a glowing Sapphira, and noted the slight frown that crossed his lordship's countenance.

"You dislike the growing friendship between Cousin Justin and my sister," she said tartly. "I assure you that you need have no fear of her trying to entrap him into declaring himself."

If his lordship was taken back by the bluntness of her words, he showed no sign of it. "My dear Karenza, I assure you that my thoughts were solely engaged in condemning the circumstances that have confined you and your sister to a rural backwater when you should have been enjoying the gaiety and interests of a London Season."

"Oh," she said, disconcerted by the depth of feeling in his voice, "then you will not wish to cast a rub in my way when I tell you that I am determined that Cressidia shall make her debut once we are out of mourning. I shall, of course, hire a house for the whole Season, and Miss Brinton will act as our chaperone."

He took her words calmly. "I agree to your desire for a London Season for Cressidia, but you are too young and too green to cope with all it entails on your own. Far better is my intention, which is to reopen the family's London residence for the benefit of you and your sisters. I have a widowed aunt, on my mother's side, who would be only too happy to introduce you to Society."

Karenza did not know whether to be pleased by his concern for them or annoyed by his calm assumption that he knew what was in their best interests, better than she herself. Nor was she agreeable to being beholdened to him for the cost of it all.

"I am grateful to you for your offer," she replied a little hesitantly, "but I do not wish for you to put yourself out on our behalf. Nor is there any justification for you to bear the expenses involved."

"Don't talk such fustian, dear cousin," he retorted. "I have my own reasons for what I do."

Karenza cast him a suspicious look. Were his reasons mainly to ensure that Sapphira should be encouraged to seek a suitor other than young Justin Mapping? Well, that would suit her, too, but it would do his lordship no harm to understand that the ladies Coningsby did not require his patronage to make their mark in polite society. The offer of the London house could be accepted without many qualms, for his lordship had already admitted to the possession of a second town residence in no less a quarter than Eaton Square.

"I do not feel we shall require the good services of your aunt. Our own dear Miss Brinton will offer us sufficient protection as our chaperone, though the use of our former London home would be most pleasing to us all, and I sincerely thank you for the kindness of your offer."

"Do you wish to live on the fringes of Society, or will only the best satisfy you?"

"Naturally I can be satisfied by only the best," she declared haughtily.

"Then let us forget Miss Brinton. It is not a kindly companion but one who is *au fait* with the world of the high ton that you require. My aunt, if she is so willing, would be an admirable person for that purpose." There was a degree of finality to his voice which forestalled further discussion on the matter.

Karenza rose gracefully to her feet. "Whilst I am appreciative of your offer, I do not know that I wish to be beholdened to your aunt or to you in this matter."

"I am sure you do not," the viscount agreed grimly. "But it will not do you any harm, either. You must try, my dear Karenza, to put the benefits that will accrue to your sisters from my patronage above your own self-conceit!"

She gave a startled gasp at the harshness of his words. "I am not being conceited," she blazed furiously. "My sisters' well-being comes first and foremost with me, and all that I do is for them."

"By which you imply that no one else has the ability to be of greater assistance to them than yourself. Well, I call that being conceited." His lordship stood, and pausing, looked down into his ward's shocked face before adding more suavely, "It is remarkable that your sisters have not made some observation on this aspect of your character. Pray, have they always been content to allow you to rule the roost?"

"You are insufferable!" Karenza all but choked on the words; her breasts rose and fell quickly in her agitation. "How dare you insult me thus!"

"It is no good looking daggers at me," said the viscount coldly. "It is I, not you, who should be feeling insulted. You have shown every disdain and lack of proper feeling whenever I have made clear my intentions to carry out my obligations as guardian to you and your sisters. You seek to spurn my desire to be of assistance in a manner that shows a sad lack of delicacy and respect. Indeed, you have revealed to me only how poorly suited you are to have sole charge of impressionable young girls. Your father acted very wisely when he placed you in my care."

Karenza, unable to find words to express her fury and dismay at such mortifying strictures being cast on her character, swung round on her heel and heedless of the surprised stares from the rest of the company, flounced out of the room.

Reaching the privacy of her own room, she paced angrily up and down, unable to compose herself, with his lordship's stinging words still ringing in her ears. How dare he speak to her thus! All her previous resentments against him came flooding back. It was his pride alone, not feelings of solicitude for his wards, that had prompted his words. To call her conceited and desiring only to dominate the family, when it was plain to all but the veriest clodpole that this was precisely what he wished to do, was beyond everything! He could not bear for her to thwart his slightest wish. Well, she would show him! Her eyes smouldered dangerously as her mind returned to her plans for gaining her complete independence of his lordship. Yet, beneath all her fury, she felt close to tears and deeply hurt, which surprised her. She had not felt so miserable since the day her father had died.

Once in bed, she was unable to relax. Her turbulent thoughts, coupled with the unusually hot stillness of the night, made sleep impossible. Eventually seeking a degree of coolness, Karenza pushed back the covers and padded softly over to the windows, pulling aside the heavy drapes to stand before the open casement. The sky was cloudless, with an almost full moon serene in its dark, velvet firmament. Below, the land slumbered. Not a sound could be heard. Only the melancholy, haunting echo of the distant chapel clock striking midnight came to her ears. The old house was enveloped in a cloak of silence, and it seemed to Karenza that she was the only living soul to whom sleep was denied.

She stood motionless, allowing the solitude of the night to ease the aching of her heart and calm her mind, watching yet not at first seeing the shadowy movement between the balustrades of the terrace below her. Almost unconsciously her eye followed the darkly clad figure which stole silently up the shallow steps, pausing for a brief moment at the top before flitting noiselessly across the flagstones and disappearing from her sight.

Shock at first held her rigid, then she heard, in the deep silence of the night, a faint scratching sound at the drawing room window below her. The soft tinkle of broken glass brought her from her trance, and her first feelings of fear gave way to a surge of unreasoning fury against the intruder.

Scarcely conscious of what she was doing, Karenza snatched up a wrap, and hastily throwing it about her shoulders, she shot barefooted from her room and moved swiftly but silently along the passage to the top of the stairs. She crept slowly down to where the stairway curved in a wide sweep; here she paused to peer uncertainly into the gloom of the hallway below. Even as she did so, she heard the faint creak of a door, and a stray beam of moonlight revealed the dark outlines of a sinister figure that appeared to gaze directly up at her.

Frightened again, Karenza shrank back into the shadows, her heart thudding as she stared with horrified eyes as the menacing shape moved slowly towards her. Step by step he came nearer to where she stood, now flattened against the wall. Her mind raced wildly seeking an escape. As she took a deep breath and prepared to utter a scream for help, her outstretched arm encountered the cold steeliness of the suit of armour that stood in the bend of the stairway and in a direct line with the figure creeping stealthily upwards. Acting instinctively, she gave it a sharp push, at the same time calling loudly, "Help! Help! Someone please help me!"

There was a thunderous sound of cascading armour, which was soon combined with the violent oaths of its unlucky recipient. There was a flash of white light and a loud report of a shot as the intruder scrambled free, his discharged pistol still being waved violently around in his hand as he sought his assailant.

Doors were being flung open and a chorus of anxious voices exclaimed in varying tones, yet it was the appearance of his lordship's figure at the far side of the hall that earned Karenza's immediate relief. He was carrying in one hand an oil lantern and in the other a rapier, whose blade gleamed threateningly in the flickering light.

"Be careful, my lord, he is armed," she called, alarmed for the viscount's safety. But her fears were unnecessary, for as his lordship advanced across the hall the dark figure of the intruder darted back through the drawing room doorway, slamming the door behind him as he went, concerned only in making his escape.

"Karenza! Where are you? Are you hurt?" Sapphira's anxious tones filled the air from the top landing as she sought the whereabouts of her twin.

Below them, the viscount raised his lantern until its beams cast themselves on Karenza's pale face as she stood clutching the banister and swaying a little unsteadily amidst the scattering of armour about her. In a few bounds, his lordship was by her side. He put a strong supporting arm around her, and gratefully, she allowed herself to lean against him, feeling strangely comforted by his presence.

"You poor girl! Lean on me," he said gently. "Did he hurt you? I heard the shots as I was leaving the library, and came as quickly as I could. Let me help you down.

Good God, he might have killed you!"

"I think his pistol discharged itself when he fell," said Karenza, allowing herself to be assisted down into the hall, where deeply concerned members of the family gathered around her, all uttering exclamations of alarm and concern as the viscount carefully eased her into a chair. Leaving her to their ministrations, Lord Darnborough retrieved his rapier and moved swiftly towards the drawing room, ignoring the cries of protest that followed him. A swift glance around the room assured him that the intruder had fled, although he was careful to check each shadowy corner. Thoughtfully, he paused by the broken window and sombrely regarded the moonlit garden beyond before returning to where his concerned wards, now joined by a shocked Miss Brinton, awaited his return.

"There is no sign of him," he said briefly. "I imagine that we have seen the last of that rogue; no doubt he will take his thievish habits elsewhere after the fright he has received here tonight."

"My love," said Miss Brinton gently to Karenza, who sat still shaken and confused, "I think it desirable for you to be in your bed. If his lordship will be so good as to assist you upstairs, I will fetch you some hot milk. Such a shock you have had, my dear, but his lordship will ensure our safety, and you have no more to worry about."

"Oh no! I cannot go up yet," protested Karenza, pressing her hand to an aching brow, wondering if she should mention her fear that Jonathan might have been the intruder's target, and not theft as supposed by the viscount.

Lord Darnborough cast her a shrewd glance. "Is there something you wish to tell me? Something concerning tonight's little episode?"

Slightly taken back by her guardian's uncanny perspicacity, Karenza gazed at him a little uncertainly, not knowing quite how to word her confession. Then deciding it would do no good for her to prevaricate—indeed, his lordship's temperament gave her no reason for believing that his sensibilities would be upset by what she had to say—she spoke without mincing her words. "Unbeknown to you, cousin, we have another guest in this house—a young man we discovered injured in the woods some two weeks ago. It is my belief that it was his life that our intruder sought tonight," she stated baldly. From beside her, Cressidia gave a little shriek of horror and looked fearfully towards the drawing room door, as if expecting the assailant to reappear.

The viscount regarded them without betraying either annoyance or astonishment, merely looking a little surprised. "You, no doubt, have good reasons for your belief. Pray, inform me as to why my unknown visitor should appear to be in any danger."

A welter of explanations assailed his lordship's ears.

"He was shot in our woods," wailed Cressidia.

"He was also savagely struck on his head," recounted Arabella, with ghoulish glee.

"There were two horses at the scene of the incident, yet no one else came to his aid," stated Drusilla in an ominous tone.

"The poor young man is obviously a gentleman, yet sadly can only recollect his first name," interposed Sapphira.

Darnborough looked a little bemused by this verbal onslaught. "What is your theory, Karenza? What is it that troubles you so? You have your own ideas, do you not?" There was no more than good-humoured concern in his voice, and she gave him a relieved smile.

"Yes," she answered slowly, and then in a firmer voice added, "my belief—and I have no proof as yet—is that Jonathan, for that is his name, is Sir Henry Faversham's grandson and heir. As you yourself suggested, the one man who would benefit from the death of the rightful heir is Beau Faversham, and he is the one who has been so anxious to inflict his company on us and is, I am quite certain, much concerned to discover the whereabouts of our unfortunate guest."

"Jonathan, Jonathan Faversham! Oh, could it be so? Yes, yes, it must be him!" Cressidia had sprung excitedly to her feet, her hazel eyes sparkling as she imagined Jonathan's reception of this wonderful news.

The viscount, who had listened in attentive silence, now spoke. "I can make no judgement until I have met the young man," he said, "but I have considerable respect for your intelligence, Karenza—although you may doubt that at times—and unusual as these circumstances appear to be, you may be assured of my support in discovering the true identity of your protégé."

Karenza gazed at him in astonishment, his attitude being so at odds with his behaviour earlier that evening that she scarcely knew how to answer him and was unable to do more than utter in a somewhat incredulous tone, "I am much obliged to you, cousin, for your kind offer."

Darnborough looked down at her, then took one of her hands into his and began to gently chafe it. "You are feeling cold! Miss Brinton, pray, fetch the hot milk that you mentioned and lace it with brandy, if you have any to hand."

"There's some in the dining room. I'll fetch it," offered Sapphira. "Cressy dear, come with me with your candle," she added, with an uncertain look at the dark shadows of the hall, while Drusilla and Arabella retreated to a quiet corner, anxious that they should not be sent back to bed.

Karenza sank back in her chair and closed her eyes. "I do not know why I should suddenly feel a little faint; I have suffered no hurt. You must think me such a weakling, my lord."

"Not at all," he responded calmly. "You have undergone a most frightening experience with admirable fortitude. Now, if you can, pray, tell me what happened; it will help you to talk about it."

As she recounted the events of that night, together with her instinctive belief that it was murder, not theft, that was the intruder's objective, Karenza was conscious of a desire to maintain the friendlier relationship that had sprung up so suddenly between her and the viscount.

"You are not angry?" she faltered at the end of her account. "We expected Jonathan to be gone before you arrived—only he did not regain his memory sufficiently for us to turn him out. With nowhere to go and no one to care for him, I could not ask him to leave."

Lord Darnborough looked more resigned than annoyed at her words. "No, I merely regret that you should have had such a poor opinion of me that you felt unable to ask for my aid in this matter. It seems that I have become the veriest of monsters in the eyes of you and your sisters."

Karenza was happily spared the necessity of answering this embarrassing statement by the reappearance of Miss Brinton with the glass of milk at the same time that Sapphira—looking somewhat flustered—moved swiftly towards them with the decanter of brandy clasped carefully in her hands.

"Where is Cressy?" Karenza asked, turning to her sister with a feeling of relief.

"Gone to see if Jonathan is all right," Sapphira replied tersely. "I did not wish her to do so, but she would not heed my objections!"

"Oh, no! She cannot have gone to his room alone!" Karenza waved away the proffered glass of milk from

Miss Brinton as she started to struggle to her feet.

She was pushed back by a firm hand. "It is obviously time that I became acquainted with my unexpected guest," stated his lordship. "Drat the girl! I had wished to leave the matter until the morning. Stay here, Karenza, and have your milk. As for Cressidia, I will deal with her!"

"Pray, do not be too severe with her; she is very concerned for the young man's safety," Karenza said, cupping her hands gratefully around the warm glass and dubiously eyeing the generous dash of brandy being added to it by her twin.

"I promise you that I will do no more than send her back to you. I have no wish to appear a greater monster than you have already painted me," said the viscount wryly.

Karenza felt herself blush at his words, while Miss Brinton earnestly sought to impress on him that she was sure his courageous assistance that evening had earned him the respect of them all. Looking singularly unimpressed by these words, his lordship departed, with a last admonition not to wait up for his return and reassurance that he would arrange for two of their stoutest footmen to patrol the terrace for the rest of the night. He would speak with Jonathan, and then they could discuss the matter further in the morning.

Within a space of several minutes a somewhat flushed-face Cressidia rejoined them to state somewhat bitterly that it was quite unnecessary for Cousin Darnborough to preach propriety to her, and as for sending her away before he had a talk with Jonathan, well anybody would think it was he who had saved the young man's life! Finding her sisters only too ready to uphold his lordship's condemnation of her actions, Cressidia would have flounced off in a high dudgeon but for a hasty plea from Karenza, in a weakened tone of voice, begging her assistance in getting to her room, as her legs felt surprisingly feeble. Concern for Karenza quickly alleviated Cressidia's injured feelings, and it was on relatively amiable terms that the sisters finally parted for what remained of the night.

Still in the hallway below, half-hidden by the shadows, Drusilla and Arabella were content to continue to discuss the night's events with a perspicacity which would have amazed their older sisters had they been privileged to overhear them.

"Cousin Darnborough is becoming much too concerned about Karenza's well-being; I think he must have fallen in love with her," Drusilla announced in a decided tone.

"Isn't he rather old for her?" Arabella protested, his thirty-two years appearing incredibly ancient to one all of fourteen.

"Some ladies prefer older men," Drusilla proclaimed in a superior tone. "I'm quite attracted to him myself, but would not wish to stand in Karenza's way," she added graciously.

"I should think not!" her sibling interjected indignantly, before adding crushingly, "besides he scarcely notices you!"

Drusilla decided to ignore this comment and instead followed a new train of thought. "I wish Karenza did not quarrel so much with him. Gentlemen do not like argumentative ladies, and it would not do if he transferred his attentions to Sapphira."

"Well, she would not have him, for she can do nothing but sigh over Cousin Justin, and he is quite besotted by her—it quite puts me out of patience with them both. The sooner they get married, the better!" Arabella frowned. "It is becoming impossible to go anywhere without meeting one or the other composing odes or talking to one about their beloved's virtues. They are in danger of becoming dead bores and not at all interested in such things as a game of shuttlecocks or jack straws!"

"So if Cressidia marries Jonathan, then we will be the only unattached young ladies in the household." Drusilla's expression brightened at this thought.

"Karenza may not be as attached to Cousin Darnborough as he is to her, and with her present no gentlemen will have regard for us, for she quite outshines us both," Arabella pointed out in a matter of fact tone, showing no resentment at this state of affairs.

Drusilla pursed her lips thoughtfully as she considered these words, then she shook her head. "No, I don't think Karenza is as indifferent to him as you suggest. It is simply that she cannot abide the thought of a stranger taking papa's place and assuming responsibility for her—but that will pass," she said airily. "You mark my words! By the time we—" But before she could enlarge on this, the exasperated voice of Miss Brinton calling them to come to bed that very instant assailed their ears, and the two young ladies, abandoning their dignity, scampered hurriedly up the stairs and disappeared rapidly in the direction of their bed chambers to the accompaniment of muttered threats as to what happened to young ladies all alone in a darkened hall with a murderous fiend on the loose—a thought guaranteed to keep them cowering safely under their sheets for what was left of the night.

11

It was not until after breakfast, a modest meal of cold meats, bread and butter and tea—the cost of the last item being no less than ten shillings and sixpence a pound, which caused Miss Brinton to gently chide Cressidia for neglecting to drink her beverage—that Jonathan joined the three elder Misses Coningsby and Miss Brinton.

A chorus of voices begged him to inform them at once of his meeting with the viscount the previous night, Cressidia pithily stating that she personally had found his lordship very unappreciative of her concern for Jonathan's safety and indignantly disclaiming his right to chide her so sharply for her presence in Jonathan's room, treating her as though she was still in leading strings.

"Oh well, I think you wrong him," Jonathan replied somewhat awkwardly, carefully avoiding his beloved's indignant gaze. "I mean that he explained, when you had left, that it was not at all the thing for you to do and was most civil towards me, offering me his hospitality and help in my misfortunes, which was more than I expected or deserved considering the circumstances."

Cressidia's obvious desire to justify her actions was curtailed by Karenza, who, wishing to turn to more serious matters, repressively informed her sister that she had been the veriest pea-goose and quelled Cressidia's protestations with a dismissive, "Then you had better return to the schoolroom to learn how to conduct yourself." She was then able to obtain a swift reassurance from Jonathan that he had not imparted to his lordship any information concerning their preparations for Buccaneer's race and that, yes, his shoulder wound was greatly eased and did little to incommode him.

There was no time for Jonathan to tell them more of his meeting with Lord Darnborough, since they were immediately joined by the viscount, looking remarkably unaffected by his exertions of the previous night, together with his nephew. Justin, after making his bow to the company, was moved to introduce himself to Jonathan, any awkwardness being quickly dispelled by the warmth of his greeting and friendly handshake. A chance remark by Justin bemoaning his failure to participate in the previous evening's excitement—particularly as he was anxious to try out his new guns, the sweetest pair of Mantons one was ever likely to find—led to an immediate response by Jonathan on the definite advantages of the New Patent Shot. In the next moment the two young men were in the depth of a discussion on the weight of shot to be used in pursuit of a variety of game.

If Cressidia greeted her guardian a little stiffly, he appeared not to notice, merely regarding her a trifle sardonically as she pointedly removed herself from his vicinity to stand as close as was possible to Jonathan.

A swift glance at his elder ward's face informed Darnborough that Karenza had not fully recovered from the events of the previous evening. There were shadows beneath the lovely eyes and a pallor to her complexion which belied her assertions of well-being, and his usually forbidding countenance relaxed as he asked her, in a friendly tone, if she had any further surprises in store for him that morning.

Karenza shot him an uneasy glance before swiftly asserting that they had quite enough to ponder on as it was and asking had he any ideas on how they could investigate the possibility that Jonathan could be none other than Sir Henry's elder grandson.

Before he could answer, the young man himself laughingly suggested that they should break into his supposed grandfather's residence and seek for clues to his identity.

"That may well be our best course," the viscount announced blandly, an amused gleam coming into his grey eyes as he watched their startled reactions.

"You! You break into Brayton Manor! You cannot be serious!" Karenza gasped in amazement.

"Why, cousin, I would not have thought you so adventurous!" There was no doubting the approving note in Cressidia's voice as she bestowed on her guardian a look of newfound respect.

"Well, I feel it may not be necessary for me to actually force my way in," his lordship commented apologetically, "for I am able, with some justification, as an acquaintance of Sir Henry's younger sister, Lady Wainforth—who indeed charged me to convey to Sir Henry innumerable messages when she learnt that I would be in this part of the world— to present myself as being duty-bound to call on him."

"That may be so," said Karenza in a puzzled tone, "but I cannot see how your visit would be of practical assistance to Jonathan, even though you share our belief that he is Sir Henry's grandson and heir."

"My dear Karenza, you cannot possibly imagine that I would indulge in mere speculation." Here Darnborough paused to open his snuffbox to take a delicate pinch. "Pray, allow me to remind you of what most fond parents have all around them, yours included, if I mistake not." His eyes drifted towards the family portrait which dominated the wall above the marbled fireplace. Painted by none other than the celebrated Thomas Gainsborough in 1785, it depicted the late Lord Darnborough as a young man, looking somewhat blue-deviled under the stern gaze of his august parents.

"Well, by Jupiter!" ejaculated Jonathan, who had obviously established a surprisingly friendly relationship with his unwitting host. "I don't think you will find a single portrait of me at Brayton Manor, even if I am one of Sir Henry's family. Your wits must be abegging my lord, if you are thinking thus."

"Not of you," explained the viscount patiently, "but one of Sir Henry and his two sons, painted when the elder one was about your own age. I have it on the good authority of Lady Wainforth, who intermittently corresponded with the errant Sylvester, that he had made some mention of his child's close resemblance to himself and his father and referred to his own portrait as a mirror-image of his son. Just a brief glimpse of this painting, to compare it with your visage, should provide us with some solid evidence on which to base your claim."

"But Beau Faversham could quite easily claim that Jonathan was no more than one of Sylvester's or even Basil's by-blows," Karenza pointed out thoughtfully, betraying a sad lack of delicacy in mentioning such matters.

Darnborough allowed only the merest twitch of his lips to betray his amusement at his ward's blunt words before adding, in a voice which silenced Jonathan's protests at being thus designated, that it would be but the first step in the battle to establish the identity of the young man and would at least indicate that they were right to connect Jonathan with the Faversham family.

"Isn't it likely that Sylvester saw in his son a resemblance because he wanted to see one?" Justin's shrewd observation succeeded in silencing them momentarily.

"That is something I shall not know until I have paid my call on Sir Henry," his lordship said dryly, casting his nephew an appreciative glance.

"Didn't Lady Wainforth know the name of the child?" asked Cressidia in a puzzled tone.

"She thought it might be David."

"Oh!" There was a keen note of disappointment in Cressidia's voice.

"Or perhaps it was Jonathan or even Goliath!" he continued. "She was not sure, since Sylvester referred to the boy in terms of endearment or by his nickname—she cannot remember which—in the few letters he wrote to her. There was some biblical connection. You must remember she is an old lady and her memory is not good. She will try to find the letters, but I do not place much hope on her doing so," the viscount stated gently. "It is likely that Sir Henry will know the answer to your question, though whether I shall have the opportunity of putting it to him remains to be seen."

"But she did mention the name Jonathan?" Cressidia repeated optimistically.

"My dear Cressidia, I thought I had already made that point clear. Yes, the name of Jonathan was mentioned, amongst others."

Darnborough took advantage of the subsequent buzz of conversation to draw nearer to Karenza and to explain that he had every intention of calling on Sir Henry that very morning. "I don't dare leave it longer, for should Sir Henry's condition worsen, it would not be possible for him to receive me. Even now, I'm not sure that I shall succeed in my mission."

"No, indeed, you cannot cause Sir Henry any distress at such a time," she returned in a concerned voice. "There must be other ways we can establish Jonathan's identity. I would be happy to leave the matter in abeyance were it not for the presence of Beau Faversham. I cannot but fear his proximity to Jonathan."

"It is certainly an interesting situation," he said, glancing at Cressidia happily conversing with Jonathan and Justin.

"You will take care, my lord, for Beau Faversham has no great liking for you."

"I doubt that he would offer me physical harm, but I appreciate your concern for me, Karenza." The unusual warmth in his eyes and voice caused Karenza to blush a rosy hue and look momentarily confused. Happily, his lordship seemed not to notice, his attention being distracted by Justin's offer to accompany him on his mission.

Darnborough shook his head. " 'Tis better if I go alone. I am more likely to be granted at least a brief meeting with Sir Henry."

"Oh well, I daresay you are right, but it is dashed unfair that you should have all the excitement," Justin stated in an aggrieved tone.

"Never mind," said his lordship, "it is important that you should remain here to receive any unwanted callers. One cannot tell if the Beau or one of his minions might pay us another visit."

"If he does, I shall be much inclined to plant him a facer, for I can't stand his primping and prancing, and he's just the type to indulge in underhand and devious ways to achieve his objectives."

"Remember, too, that he may be willing to use murder to accomplish his aims," Darnborough added dryly.

Sapphira, who had silently joined them, gave a gasp of horror at his words and raised frightened eyes to Justin's face. "Oh, pray, do not leave us to the mercies of such a creature, I beg of you."

Justin immediately assured her that nothing would tear him from her side, while Cressidia, anxious that Jonathan should not appear in a lesser light, loftily announced that Jonathan would stand guard until his lordship's return.

"My dear Cressy, Jonathan will do no such thing," said Karenza dampingly. "It is essential not only that he should remain out of the sight of any visitor, but that he should also assist me . . . eh, with certain undertakings," she ended vaguely, carefully avoiding his lordship's speculative gaze. Happily for her peace of mind, the viscount made no comment beyond a vague admonition to her not to accost any strangers on horseback.

"You are quite abominable!" hissed Karenza in an undertone, once sure that none were listening to them.

"Oh, surely not," he answered, smiling down into her indignant green eyes. "I am but overly concerned that you should not fall into low company through your friendly nature," he added blandly.

"Odious creature! I am surprised that you have the audacity to even refer to your shocking want of conduct, Mister Marcus! Now I wish you will stop funning and tell me in all seriousness whether you share my feeling that Beau Faversham knows that we are hiding Jonathan. I wish I could discover his intentions."

His eyes became suddenly thoughtful, searching her face. "One would have to be positively bird-witted to ignore making the assumption that he knows Jonathan is in or near the Hall, my dear Karenza, and since you have had the good sense to apply to me for assistance in investigating the mystery of Jonathan's identity, you must abide by my insistence that you do not, under any circumstances, take any action which could endanger your well-being or that of your sisters. Next time you catch a glimpse of a possible intruder, you lock your door and ring for one of the servants to come and fetch me. 'Tis sheer folly to imagine that you are capable of dealing with such a situation on your own."

He ended on a note of harshness, but Karenza had not missed the depth of concern for her in his voice, and touched by it, bit back the angry retort which had sprung to her lips. Instead, she replied in a prosaic and kindly voice, "Very proper. I must try and remember your wishes in the unlikely event of a further visitation. 'Tis a pity that I have such a shocking memory."

"Did your father ever mention a desire to wring your neck, Karenza?" his lordship asked carefully.

Laughter sprang into her expressive eyes. "Not that I can recall," she said demurely. "Papa always insisted that I did not follow the missish ways of my contemporaries—in fact, he would box my ears if I jumped at the noise of a gun or feared to put my horse to a fence when out hunting. Mama said he regarded me more as a son than a daughter." She sighed. "I do not know if that was true, but we were very close to each other."

He had been listening to her in amusement, but at that his expression altered. "You have been more than fortunate in your parents in that you have been loved and cherished," he said gently. "That can never be taken away from you."

"Perhaps not, but," she added wryly, "I cannot ignore his weaknesses; he squandered our inheritance, bringing ninepence to nothing. In my grandfather's time, this estate was one of the best in the county; now it lies neglected and rundown, whilst we, his daughters, are left in very straightened circumstances. Still, I must not prittle-prattle about what is past; it is the future which is important now."

At these words his lordship frowned, uneasily aware that he, who had so unwillingly assumed the responsibility for Karenza and her sisters, was now anxious to do all in his power to help her. For the first time in his life he felt a degree of uncertainty, not wishing to arouse Karenza's incomprehensible hostility to his desire to relieve her of all financial hardship, knowing that the merest mention of doing so would be enough to bring an icy coldness to the lovely green eyes and a withdrawal of her present friendliness. It was a salutary experience for one whose fortune had ensured him avowals of undying affection from every female to whom he had deigned to show the slightest interest. For the first time in his life a girl, and a young, green girl at that, showed not the smallest desire to win his favour. Indeed, he suspected that she even went out of her way to cross him at the slightest provocation.

These thoughts were interrupted by Cressidia pointedly reminding him that if he wished to reach Sir Henry's residence before noon, he should waste no time in sending his orders to the stables to saddle up his horse and informing him that since his own mounts now had arrived at the Hall, it would be quicker for him to ride than to take his curricle.

"Very true; I will leave at once," Darnborough said, almost glad to be spared the necessity of replying to Karenza's words. Such unexpected meekness caused his eldest ward to glance at him with suspicion, but he met her look with one of unruffled good humour before requesting directions to Brayton Manor.

His departure was a signal for Miss Brinton to remember that she had not as yet consulted the housekeeper on the vexed question of whether or not to engage another underhousemaid to assist with the additional domestic chores arising from the presence of the new viscount and his nephew. As she bustled from the room, Justin seized the opportunity to persuade Sapphira to take a gentle perambulation through the rose garden, while Cressidia, swiftly forestalling any attempt by Karenza to part her from Jonathan, announced that they would await her eldest sister in the stable yard, for she would surely wish to change into her riding clothes before beginning Buccaneer's training session.

Appreciative of her sister's tactics, Karenza did no more than indicate her consent to these arrangements and withdrew to her bedchamber to don more suitable apparel for her activities.

Hardly had she reappeared than she was accosted outside her room by a bristling Datchett.

"I have to inform you, Miss Karenza, that there is a person requiring to speak with you. He is awaiting you in the Great Hall." There was no mistaking the disdain in the butler's voice, which indicated his strong disapproval of the new arrival. "A rather low type," he added in answer to his mistress's look of surprised enquiry.

"Are you sure it is not Lord Darnborough whom he seeks?" she asked doubtfully.

"Unfortunately, he mentioned you by name, miss. I did suggest that he should await his lordship, but this he has refused to do. Shall I say you are not at home?"

"No. I shall only be plagued by curiosity as to the reason for his visit. Show him into the library."

"Very well, Miss Karenza, but I shall be in attendance outside the door should you have need of me." On this ominous note Datchett withdrew, leaving a puzzled Karenza to come slowly down the staircase a few moments later.

Datchett was not the only person to look askance upon the person who swung round to meet Karenza as she entered the library. She herself was taken back by the sight of the stocky, middle-aged man, whose homely features were not enhanced by small, darting brown eyes beneath his close crop of wiry, ginger hair flecked with grey. A smile, which failed to reach his eyes, did nothing to improve his visage as he made her an awkward bow.

"You wish to speak to me?" Karenza allowed her surprise to show in her voice. "Who are you?"

"Ben Drover, ma'am. You being the Honourable Miss Coningsby who lives in this ken," he replied with a comprehensive sweep of his hand. His accent was not that of a local man, more that of a Londoner, but his apparel suggested a countryman, with his broad-brimmed hat, gaitered legs and short, wide coat with its large pockets sagging shapelessly from the constant thrust of impatient hands.

"I see you know me. I'm afraid that you have the advantage of me in that respect."

"I can tell, ma'am, that you're a trifle curious to know what my lay is, in a manner of speaking," he replied amiably.

"Your lay?" repeated Karenza in a bewildered tone.

"I'm not one for talking slummery, miss, and I'll smack calfskin that what I have to tell you is nobbut the truth." He paused to fish inside his inner pocket, while Karenza continued to gaze at him in blank astonishment, not understanding a word he had said. He drew out a small notebook and handed it to her.

Without speaking she opened it and glanced down at the flyleaf, which bore its owner's name and underneath the words that clearly indicated his occupation, "Occurrence Book." "You're a Bow Street runner!" The words burst from her lips. "But what can you wish to speak to me about?" There was no doubting the puzzlement in her voice or expression.

Ben Drover cast her a shrewd glance before saying in a confiding tone, "Well, ma'am, it concerns the present whereabouts of a bridle-cove, Dan Gunn himself, no less. Or perhaps what I should say,"—he hastily corrected himself—"and stand to, is that there is a dangerous highwayman known to be in this area and,"—here he paused before adding slowly—"I don't wish to offend you, ma'am, but it is believed that you might have given him succour—not knowing, of course, that he was destined for the nubbing-cheat."

Karenza appeared to show little interest in his words. "I cannot imagine where you have obtained such misinformation. Your brains must be positively addled if you believe that I or any member of this household could be so involved with a common felon. I find the very suggestion absurd and can only suggest that—" But what she was about to suggest was not to be revealed, for as she spoke from the direction of the garden came the harsh explosion of a gun followed by a piercing scream.

Without a word the man with her sprang into action. Pushing Karenza to one side as Datchett burst into the room, Ben Drover took a flying leap through the open window, disappearing in the direction of the rose garden. With fear in her heart, Karenza scrambled frantically after him, leaving Datchett to follow at a more decorous speed.

Sapphira's wild sobs guided Karenza to the spot where her shocked gaze alighted on the crumbled figure of Justin, stretched unmoving on the lawn, with Sapphira bowed over him. There was no sign of Ben Drover as Karenza hurried to her side, while others from the house converged upon them both, though—Karenza noted with a feeling of relief—Jonathan was not among them.

Karenza wasted no time in questioning her distraught twin. A rapid check of Justin's wound revealed profuse bleeding from his head, which made it difficult to judge the extent of his injuries. Once more Karenza found herself guiding the efforts of the servants to raise the injured man and bear him gently to the house, at the same time assuring her sister that their cousin still lived. A string of orders issued from her lips, and within moments two of the grooms were spurring their way down the drive—one to fetch the doctor and the other to inform Lord Darnborough of the latest happening at his country residence.

If Karenza had not been sure before of Sapphira's feelings for Justin Mapping, she now was left in no doubt. Lifting tear-drenched eyes to gaze into the anxious and sympathetic face of her sister, Sapphira's broken words tore at her heart. "We love each other, Karenza, we love each other! Just before he was shot, Justin told me he had fallen in love with me from the very moment we met. He proposed to me, Karenza, and I accepted him! I never realised just how much I do love him until this moment, and now he may be taken from me! He mustn't die! Oh, how could such a dreadful thing happen to him! Who could wish him such ill!"

Feeling it was not the moment to confide in her sister that the would-be assassin had possibly mistaken Justin for Jonathan, Karenza put her arm about her sister's slender waist and gave her a little hug, saying with forced cheerfulness as she gently guided her towards the house, "Come now, my dearest, do not let yourself despair of Justin's recovery. These head wounds often look a great deal worse than they are. You must have courage and present to your beloved a confident and cheerful visage, lest you add to his fears. Now wipe away your tears, for we have work to do." And without further talk the two sisters passed into the house.

12

Never had Karenza felt such exquisite relief as she did at the sight of her guardian as he paused at the entrance to Justin's bedchamber before coming silently forward to stand grim-faced, looking down at his nephew.

"This is Lord Darnborough, Dr Beech," she murmured, continuing to remove the bloodstained swabs as fast as the physician discarded them cleaning the freshly stitched wound. Sapphira continued to gaze in silent anguish as she chafed Justin's cold hands.

The doctor checked his actions and directed a searching look at the viscount from beneath his bushy brows. "His uncle, are you not? Well, there is no need for you to fear the worse. He is not about to stick his spoon to the wall; though I'll wager many a coach wheel that it was more by luck than by judgement he escaped with his life."

"So it would appear," said Darnborough coolly. "How badly is my nephew injured?"

"The shot grazed the side of his skull. It looks much worse than it is, my lord. He's lost a lot of blood and suffered a concussion, but there is no serious damage done. He'll have a bad headache of course. I've had to put in a dozen stitches, but I've dosed him with laudanum to ease the shock. What he needs now is rest and quiet. Keep him warm, and if he should be at all feverish, give him

146

a draught of saline; I'll have a bottle made up and send my assistant with it." He paused and eyed Karenza half-humorously. "Perhaps I had better prepare a wide range of remedies for this household; there seems to be a somewhat abnormal demand for the treatment of gun wounds at Darnborough Hall."

"Rest assured, doctor, I have every intention of bringing these nefarious attacks to an end," said his lordship grimly. "Tomorrow I shall send for the runners."

A startled gasp came from Karenza's lips. "I'm afraid one is already here—at least he was with me at the time that Justin was shot. I had forgotten all about him. I believe he went in pursuit of the assailant. I hope no harm has come to him. Oh dear, the cat will be in the cream pot if he finds Jonathan. I must go and—"

"If," interrupted his lordship, "you think I am going to let you disappear in search of a complete stranger, who you tell me is in pursuit of some murderous assailant, then you must have windmills in your head, my girl." He strode to the bellpull and gave it a violent tug before turning round to meet the worried look of his ward. "You are to remain with your patient and Sapphira, whilst I—" What his lordship's intentions were, were to remain in abeyance as Datchett made a dignified entry.

"You rang, my lord?"

"I am informed that we have a Bow Street runner on the grounds. Assemble some of the footmen and grooms to search the area with me. He must be found before he discovers the whereabouts of Mr Jonathan. Also warn the servants that they will incur my serious displeasure if they should mention to him that young man's presence among us."

The firm, authorative voice appeared to have little effect on its recipient, who, indicating his stern disapproval of such goings on in a gentleman's residence, merely said,

"There is no need for your lordship to disturb himself on the matter. That *person*," and there was no mistaking the disdain in Datchett's voice, "is awaiting your lordship's pleasure in the small saloon, and," he added with some relish, "looking as melancholy as a gib cat."

"In that case, I'll go to him immediately. I will say good-bye to you now, Doctor Beech, and ask you to forgive my lack of courtesy in not asking you to partake of a glass of madeira with me. No doubt you will be with us again tomorrow, and I shall look for the pleasure of your company then." With a last look at his nephew and a half-bow towards Karenza and Sapphira, the viscount left the room, followed closely by Datchett.

The doctor packed his instruments into his bag, saying comfortingly as he did so, "Well, I don't expect any change in this young man's condition, but should you have any cause for alarm, send someone for me and I will come at once."

"If he wakes, shall I give him anything?" asked Sapphira in an anxious voice, still not moving from the bedside where she had been ever since they had placed the bleeding figure there.

"He should not wake, but if he does so, you may give him some barley water or lemonade but no wine, mind you. I'll visit him again in the morning, when he should have his wits about him, even if his head feels sore."

Downstairs, Lord Darnborough paused at the entrance of the saloon. "You are waiting to see me?" he enquired gently.

At these softly spoken words, the sturdy man spun round to face the speaker, behind whom the disapproving face of Datchett could be clearly seen.

"I'd as lief as not talk in front of old muffin-face there, my lord. That is, if you be the new viscount and owner of this ken," Drover said bluntly, showing a sad lack of respect for his betters, as Datchett was quick to inform him in freezing tones.

"Mum your dubber, you bacon-slicer! I've got business with this gentry mort which ain't to be discuss'd in front of any silly nodcock," the runner exclaimed impatiently.

A faint smile tugged at the corners of his lordship's mouth as he glanced at the indignant face of his majordomo.

"That will be all, Datchett. You may go," Darnborough said kindly to his highly irate servitor, who departed with a stiff bow to his master, contemptuously ignoring his lowly tormentor.

"Now, what is it that you wish to say to me? For I do assure you that I am Lord Darnborough and the owner of, er, what you call 'this ken.' "

"I won't try to bamboozle you, my lord. There's one in this area who squeaked the beef on the fact you was hiding a wanted felon—a stub-faced cull known as Dan Gunn, one I very much want to get my fambles on, seeing as how he put a bullet into one of my men, which makes him a prime candidate for the nubbing-cheat—and all the more dangerous for that reason." Drover surveyed the viscount with an unblinking stare.

Darnborough appeared unmoved as he withdrew his snuffbox and casually took a pinch before saying coolly, "It is not my custom to associate with highwaymen, nor could I imagine any circumstances which would make me wish to assist one. Your informer must have been on the wrong side of the hedge when brains were given out if he believes in what he has said. But if I mistake not, you do not share his suspicions."

"I don't know what I think," Drover answered in an exasperated tone. "He could be a flying-porter. Lord knows we get enough of them trying to get money from the victims of robberies by giving false information that they claim will lead to an arrest. And I must say I don't see you as one to hobnob with bridle-culls. Besides, there's your own nephew lying shot. 'Taint likely you'd be giving aid to his attacker—that's if they are one and the same man."

"But are they?" the viscount asked gently.

There was a short silence, while Drover considered this question. "I think you have something to tell me, my lord," he finally said, fixedly regarding the viscount. "Maybe I was mistook in believing you had nothing to do with Dan Gunn."

"You need have no worry on that score," said Darnborough calmly. "In fact, I very much doubt that he is in this part of the country at all. Apart from your one informant have you been able to obtain any other evidence of Gunn's whereabouts?"

The runner slowly shook his head. "There's not been a whisper of a toby man in the area, but that don't always mean there ain't one around. I'll tell you to your head, my lord, that people keep their chaffers closed in these parts."

The viscount breathed a secret sigh of relief before asking nonchalantly, "Do you have a description of this fellow you seek?"

"In a manner of speaking, since no two persons say the same. He's flash-gentry, a real out-and-outer. Not over big, slimlike, must be twenty-four or -five; good-looking in a way, or so his female victims say. Mind you, he don't let any cast their ogles on his face, all muffled up he is, but they swear he's got brownish eyes and hair—that much they could see—and you know how women notice such details."

There was nothing in Darnborough's face to indicate how disconcerting this information was to him. Giving a mental shrug, he turned his attention to dispelling his visitor's obvious suspicions that somehow the members of Darnborough Hall were involved in nefarious activities.

Having no evidence of Beau Faversham's involvement to present the runner, and anxious to divert the fellow's attention from his wards, his lordship had few scruples in impugning his nephew's character. "I can give you no help concerning your Gunn friend, but I am certain that he is not the same man as attacked my nephew. For if I mistake not, his assailant was some village swain who objected to young Justin's pursuit of his ladylove. He is, I fear, somewhat inclined to trifle with the affections of attractive village maidens." His lordship met Drover's suspicious gaze with cool indifference. He then continued to discourse amiably on the reprehensible conduct of the younger generation until the runner bluntly interrupted him.

"No doubt your lordship also knows the name of the said party."

"I cannot be certain, and of course I have no evidence for my beliefs," the viscount stated carefully, "but I am inclined to suspect that my nephew had a tendre for a certain, er, Maggie . . . um . . . Baker. I believe she is the daughter of the local blacksmith. I am sure Justin was no more than the victim of a righteously angry lovelorn youth," he added mendaciously, "and has come by his just deserts."

"Well now, you're mighty understanding of an attack on your nephew. There's not many men, particularly gentry, who would take it so calmly," said Drover, his voice heavy with disbelief as he gazed with some perplexity into his lordship's face. "And I seem to have the notion that you'll not be wanting any charges to be brought against this rustic," he added caustically.

"I would prefer to avoid the scandal it would entail," Darnborough stated in an apologetic tone.

"Dang me, if you ain't a rum one!" Drover observed, surprisingly unperturbed by his lordship's attitude. "Since there be no further need for me here, I'd best lope off."

Refusing his lordship's offer of a gig to take him to the village, saying he had a hired horse to hand, which he castigated as the greatest slug over which he had ever crossed a leg in his life, Drover took leave of the viscount in an affable manner, adding that he intended to stay in the district for a few more days and would perhaps have the honour of meeting his lordship again.

No sooner had Ben Drover made his departure than Datchett begged to inform his lordship that all the family, together with Mr Jonathan, awaited him in the dining room, where a light repast was being served.

No sooner had the viscount entered the room than he was bombarded with a pelter of questions, which he checked with a raised hand before asking Karenza the latest information on Justin's well-being.

When satisfied that Justin's condition need cause no real concern, he proceeded to enlighten them with details of his meeting with Ben Drover. Sapphira's indignant protests at the slur cast on Justin's character were swept away by the general approval of the viscount's conduct by the rest of the family, who were quick to grasp the significance of the similarity in appearance of Dan Gunn and Jonathan.

With her eyes brimming with mirth, Karenza addressed him in an admiring tone. "Well, I never thought to hear you utter such a plumper about your own nephew, but it will do very well, very well indeed, cousin."

"Surely it would be best if Mr Drover was made aware of our suspicions concerning Beau Faversham," commented Sapphira, still unhappy with the insinuation that Justin was dangling after the lowly but lovely Maggie Baker.

The viscount shot her a not-unsympathetic look before saying reflectively, "I cannot but feel that Jonathan's position would be a difficult one if he came within the ambit of the law. Just consider, it would be the case of one man's word that he was not the much-wanted Dan Gunn, though his looks match the description given of the wanted felon. In addition to which he would then have the authorities believe that he had lost his memory and could not prove that he was elsewhere at the times of the various holdups. It would only need one person to proclaim him as the rogue who held him or her up—and I would not put it past our friend Basil Faversham to provide such a witness—and Jonathan would be en route to the gallows."

At these words Cressidia's face whitened and she gave a convulsive shudder, clutching at Jonathan's arm as she did so. The young man himself gave a wry smile and patted her hand gently before saying with forced jocularity, "It's a deuce of a puzzle to know what to do next, and no doubt I shall find myself in queer stirrups if that redbreast catches me. But I shall come about somehow, have no fear of that." Yet his worried eyes belied the confidence of his words.

"Did your lordship succeed in your mission to Sir Henry this morning?" Miss Brinton's enquiry recalled to their minds the reason for the viscount's absence earlier that day.

Questioning eyes turned eagerly towards Darnborough.

"Unhappily, Sir Henry was not well enough to receive me." There was no doubting the disappointment that greeted these words. "I was, however," he continued smoothly, "offered refreshments in the drawing room before my departure, and whilst partaking of a glass of excellent madeira, had the opportunity to closely inspect the family portrait mentioned by Lady Wainforth." The viscount regarded Jonathan thoughtfully before turning once more to his audience, who was hanging breathlessly on his every word. "The likeness was quite remarkable," he said softly. "There is not the slightest doubt in my mind that Jonathan is related to the Faversham family, the only questions being what is that relationship? And can it be proved?"

Above the buzz of chatter that greeted these revelations, Cressidia urgently demanded if cousin Darnborough had also discovered the Christian name of Sylvester's only son.

"Knowing that I could be expected to have done so, I took the precaution of asking the butler if Sir Henry's elder grandson had arrived," said Darnborough, "and received the reply that 'Mr Jonathan was expected daily!'" He was obliged to repeat word for word the conversation he had had with Sir Henry's devoted retainer until he could divert attention from it by pointing out there was nothing more he could add for their edification and that he was devilishly hungry.

Karenza, who had been gazing at him with something akin to admiration, beseeched the present company to allow his lordship to stave off the possibility of fainting from hunger by partaking of some of the cold meats, cakes, jellies and fruit which constituted the midday meal, recommending to him, in a kindly tone, the ham that had a delicious honey flavour. But before Darnborough had time to consume a single mouthful, Karenza was asking him if he had met Beau Faversham again at Brayton Manor.

"He was not at home," he said resignedly, "nor did I show any desire to learn of his whereabouts, for it would no doubt soon reach his ears if I revealed any untoward interest in him. I do not wish him to know that I am curious about his activities in this part of the world."

"Then, we cannot be sure if it was he or his man who shot Justin this morning," she said. "Oh, how vexing it is!"

"Very disobliging of him," the viscount responded sardonically. "Still, we cannot expect the assailant to have left his calling card."

A worried frown crossed Karenza's brow, and she fixed her eyes a little anxiously upon his face. "Do you think we should inform Lady Mapping of Justin's injury?"

"Why?" he asked shortly.

She gazed at him in astonishment. "Well, she is his mother."

"That point is not in dispute," he commented dryly.

Karenza gave a little gurgle of laughter before adding in a serious tone, "If it happened to one of my sisters and I was not informed, I would be most upset and angry. But I daresay you know your sister best, and I do not wish to interfere in your family affairs."

At these words the viscount, who was about to reject any attempt to bring Lady Mapping—and possibly Sir Frederick as well—to impinge on the already complex situation at Darnborough Hall, paused before saying a trifle wryly, "I was somehow under the impression that we were all one family, even if a little remote in our connections."

Karenza flushed and looked a little embarrassed before saying awkwardly, "I did not mean to sound disobliging, nor do I repudiate our relationship, but there is no point in pretending that we are not more or less strangers, and as such Lady Mapping can have but little interest in our affairs."

"I can assure you that my sister is more than a little concerned about you," he interjected. "In fact, she shares your feeling that I should have made myself available to visit Darnborough Hall at a much earlier date. Nor should I like you to think she is not a devoted mother. Indeed, it would be hard for her to tear herself away from the rest of her progeny to come here—and I'm damned if I want the whole family descending on us!"

"No, indeed it would be too much!" said Karenza feelingly, knowing that the organization of such a houseful would fall on her shoulders, in spite of her determination to have nothing to do with the daily routine of the household.

Things had not quite worked out as she intended in that respect, what with the problems over Jonathan and Justin. This put her in mind of Sapphira's feelings for young Mr Mapping. Then, stifling her own inclination to use the latest event as an excuse for sending Justin off home, Karenza reiterated her concern for Lady Mapping's maternal instincts and pointed out that Lord Darnborough would be quite justified in indicating that, while his sister's presence would be welcome, should she feel the need to see her beloved offspring, circumstances did not enable his lordship to extend the invitation to the rest of his nephews and nieces.

The viscount regarded his ward thoughtfully. "I will grant that you may be right in this matter," he said at last. "I will arrange for a letter to catch the mail tomorrow. A groom can ride to Huntingdon as soon as it is light. I believe the coach leaves at seven in the morning, but it will take at least two days to reach her. By the time she is ready to leave her home, Justin will be as right as a trivet."

"You can tell her that, for I've no doubt it will be of comfort to Lady Mapping and may persuade her that there is no call for her to journey here," Karenza replied, knitting her brows as she pondered whether or not it would be to Sapphira's advantage for Justin's mother to meet her. Surely she would come to approve of a match between the two once she came to know Sapphira, for no one but a complete gudgeon could possibly believe her twin was on the catch for a rich husband. In any event, she would be less inclined to talk against Sapphira if made aware of her son's misfortune than if left in ignorance until a much later date.

At this point Sapphira flitted away in the wake of Miss Brinton in order to reassure herself of the well-being of the latest invalid, while Jonathan stretched out a hand to select a peach, carefully pinching it to see if it was ripe before enquiring of Karenza whether she wished to ride with him that afternoon. "I am at your service, as always," he said with a mischievous look, "unless you, my lord," he added, looking at the viscount, "feel there is something I should be doing to effect my claim as the lost heir."

"There is little that can be done at the moment," the viscount said slowly. "I must, however, insist that you avoid exposing yourself to unnecessary danger. Remember, you are the Beau's target, and it would be unwise to go riding around the countryside. There is also the added danger of meeting Ben Drover. He is more intelligent than he appears, and I am by no means certain that he has accepted my story concerning Justin's assailant. I believe he still may be seeking Dan Gunn in this area."

Jonathan raised his eyes from the peach he was skinning. "I must go riding," he protested.

"Why is it so important to you? Indeed, I would say it would be better for your shoulder if you avoided such activities for the present." There was no denying the good sense of Darnborough's words.

Jonathan exchanged a worried look with Karenza, which was not missed by his lordship.

"I shall go and exercise Buccaneer in the paddock behind the stable; you can come and talk to me there," Karenza said smoothly. "I should imagine that it would be quite safe for you to do so. Later, Cousin Darnborough will undoubtedly inform us of the next step we must take in connection with establishing your identity." She gave him a whimsical smile.

His lordship regarded her speculatively for several moments before saying in fading tones, "Your faith in my abilities positively overwhelms me, my dear Karenza. What have I done to earn such approbation?"

She could not help laughing at his gently satirical words. "Oh, I am sure you will think of something, cousin," she paused before adding in a sugar-sweet voice, "after all, you would not wish me to advise you on what to do, being but a mere female!"

"Doing it rather too brown!" his lordship retorted. "I shall remind you of what you have said!"

"I am quite sure you will," she answered gaily. "Now do come along, Jonathan, and you too, Cressy dear, and we will leave Cousin Darnborough in peace." Without further to-do, the three of them left the room.

"I wonder what crack-brained idea is flitting through that lovely little head?" the viscount asked himself as he gazed thoughtfully after them before turning once more to seeking a solution to the problems presented by the Faversham family.

🍃 13

Little occurred to disturb the quiet tenor of life over the next four days, much to the relief of all concerned.

Justin made good progress, and apart from the bandage around his head, showed few signs of his ordeal, while Sapphira made little attempt to hide her loving concern for his well-being.

Karenza continued to spend much time with Jonathan training Buccaneer. With the day of the great race fast approaching—indeed that coming Thursday would witness the success or failure of her plan—she was strongly inclined to abandon the whole scheme, but her pride would not let her. Instead, she spent every free moment riding the great stallion under Jonathan's tuition.

Absorbed in her preparations, Karenza failed to notice his lordship's frowning glances that followed her frequent departures with Jonathan. She would, indeed, have been more than a little surprised had she been made aware of Darnborough's growing ire at her apparent preference for the younger man's company. Thus, she received with annoyed astonishment his censure on her lack of propriety in insisting on dispensing with a chaperone on these occasions.

"Oh what fustian!" she replied with indignation when he remarked on this oversight. "You are being quite absurd to imagine that I have need to be accompanied thus in my own home. I am no young miss fresh from the schoolroom!"

"Don't nauseate me with nonsensical assertions about your age!" Darnborough retorted with acerbity. "You may be mistress of Darnborough Hall, but you are, nevertheless, a very green girl, Karenza!"

Provoked by what seemed to her his unnecessary arrogance, and determined to give his lordship a sharp setdown, Karenza made no attempt to control her annoyance. "Firstly, I would inform you, my lord, that I no longer consider myself mistress of what is now your house," she replied disdainfully. "That is a privilege to be bestowed on the unfortunate female who is misguided enough to accept your offer of marriage. And secondly, I do not accept your authority to govern my actions!"

Before Darnborough could speak again, Karenza spun on her heel and departed, a figure of outraged dignity, leaving the viscount gazing after her, looking more than a little exasperated by her repudiation of his right to concern himself with her well-being.

Karenza was still feeling ruffled when she met Jonathan after luncheon at the stables, therefore, she decided to punish his lordship by spending longer than she had at first intended on Buccaneer's training session, absenting herself until almost five o'clock.

She was thus unaware that Cressidia was also missing. That young lady, impatient with their lack of progress in establishing Jonathan's rightful place in Society, had decided to take matters into her own hands and had departed in the household chaise in the direction of Brayton Manor in the innocent company of her two younger sisters and Miss Denny, the latter being sadly ignorant of their true destination. Thus it was that Karenza was entirely unprepared for the sight of her sisters and their preceptress in an unfamiliar carriage being drawn to a halt by the front portico by none other than Beau Faversham!

At the sound of the hoof beats, the Beau turned sharply, still holding the reins and staring with narrowing eyes at the two riders as they abruptly wheeled their horses away from him and rode swiftly in the direction of the stables.

It was left to the viscount to discover the reason for the sudden appearance of Beau Faversham on the scene, as the party made its entry.

"Oh, Cousin Darnborough, Mr Faversham has been so kind as to drive us home after a wheel on our chaise became loose and we were forced to seek assistance at Brayton Manor," Cressidia trilled in an unusually gushing tone, which caused his lordship to cast her a suspicious glance before expressing his gratitude to the Beau.

"I am much obliged to you, my dear Percy. I fear my young wards have imposed a great deal on your good nature," he stated in languid tones. "I trust you have not been greatly incommoded by them."

The Beau stood looking at him narrowly before he replied. "I am happy to have been of service to the ladies. It was indeed most fortunate for them that the er . . . accident should have occurred so close to the manor." His lordship did not fail to detect the note of skepticism in the Beau's voice, but he did not allow his awareness to show as he cordially invited their rescuer to accompany him to the adjoining saloon to partake of suitable refreshment.

The young ladies reiterated their thanks in effusive tones, as a flustered Miss Denny reminded them to make their curtsies and withdraw, adding in a rather tremulous voice, "I fear, Mr Faversham, that we have imposed too much on your kindness this afternoon, and I feel myself much at fault for allowing myself to be persuaded to make our little expedition."

"Expedition?" The viscount raised an enquiring eyebrow.

"To see the crusader's tomb in the chapel near Brayton Manor," interjected Cressidia in a pious tone.

"A tomb?" said Darnborough incredulously.

"A most interesting monument," Cressidia stated curtly. "Did you not think so?" she demanded of her sisters.

When their elder sister spoke in that tone of voice it was unwise to disagree with her, and both young ladies hastily asserted that it had been a highly edifying experience, a view which caused their harassed governess to look at them in amazement.

"It was as we were leaving the chapel that Jenkins informed me that the chaise's wheel had all but removed itself from its axle, thus leaving us with no alternative but to impose ourselves on Sir Henry's household." Cressidia paused to shoot a swift glance at her guardian, who stiffened slightly at these words. But if he wondered why a young stableboy instead of the family coachman should be driving the Coningsby ladies, he made no effort to pursue the matter, accurately deducing that Jenkin's presence had been to ensure cooperation in the removal of the chaise's wheel at the appropriate moment.

Relieved by the comprehending gleam in her cousin's eye, Cressidia was encouraged to conclude her saga. "Sadly, Sir Henry was not well enough to receive us, but his housekeeper, Mrs Glossop, looked after us very well and would have arranged for Sir Henry's coachman to drive us home, but Mr Faversham insisted on bringing us himself."

"An unmerited kindness," his lordship commented dryly.

Ignoring these civilities, the Beau withdrew his snuffbox from his pocket and opened its lid with a practised flick, saying as he did so, "I note you have an additional guest in your house, Marcus. When I saw him with Miss Karenza just now, I could swear that I knew him. Pray, tell me who he is." He took a delicate pinch of snuff, but as he inhaled it, his eyes fastened unblinkingly on the viscount.

"I am sure that you do know him," Darnborough answered easily, "for he is often in Society, and you must have met him frequently."

"Then you must forgive my shocking memory for names, for I cannot recollect his at this moment," the Beau answered smoothly.

"Why, my dear fellow, it is only my nephew, Justin Mapping, my sister's eldest son," said Darnborough coolly.

"I could have sworn this fellow had dark hair, and Justin is quite fair, as I recall," the Beau observed, the cold anger in his hard eyes belying the amiability of his words.

The challenge in no way disconcerted his lordship. "I fear it was no more than a trick of sun and shadows, for as you so well remember, Justin takes after his father in his fairness. Now, do let us go in and try some excellent sherry that Datchett has discovered for me in the cellar. I am sure my wards and Miss Denny will excuse us."

Miss Denny, her attention thus claimed, begged the girls to take their leave, and in a confused welter of half-completed sentences, they finally withdrew, leaving the viscount to discuss the merits of the various wines at Darnborough Hall with the highly suspicious Mr Faversham.

Once free of their company, Cressidia fled in search of Justin to implore him to remain out of sight until their visitor had departed, for one glimpse of his bandaged head would undo all the viscount's good work.

She found her target in the company of Sapphira, Miss Brinton and an exasperated Karenza. Karenza rounded on her as soon as she entered the small side saloon in the west wing, demanding to know what manner of activity she had been indulging in to bring about the presence of the Beau at such an inopportune moment.

Breathlessly, Cressidia recounted the events of the afternoon, ending triumphantly, "And I had the cosiest chat with Mrs Glossop, who has been at the manor for years and years and knew Sylvester and his brother and was able to tell me much about the family."

"Well, what did that achieve, except for the Beau to know for certain that Jonathan is still with us?" Karenza said, concerned by this event in a manner which she could not explain to her sisters.

Cressidia took a deep breath before imparting her information in almost a whisper, as though afraid that the Beau would somehow overhear what she was about to say.

"She said that Sir Henry had received a letter from his lawyer." She paused and eyed her attentive audience with a look of smug satisfaction before continuing. "And it gave details of the unknown grandson, including his description and mentioning that he had inherited a family trait which would undoubtedly endear him to his grandfather, since Sir Henry also possessed it," she ended dramatically.

Deeply appreciative of her sister's enjoyment of her moment of triumph, Karenza cast her an open look of admiration, saying at the same time, "That was very well done, Cressy dear."

"Such ingenuity of thought to take you there," stated Sapphira, regarding her younger sibling with considerable respect.

Nor was Justin backward in expressing his relief at gaining more definite evidence concerning Jonathan's identity. "Your achievement puts us to shame, cousin," he said with a charming smile. "But do not, I beg of you, keep us any longer in suspense. Tell us immediately—what was the description given of the grandson, and more important, what is this 'family trait' that seems so likely to enhance his standing with Sir Henry?"

Cressidia looked momentarily disconcerted. "Well, Mrs Glossop did not actually know the details," she said reluctantly. "But I am sure it will not be difficult to discover them," she added with airy confidence.

"How?" demanded Karenza bluntly, with an uneasy suspicion that her sister might well have some other adventurous scheme to carry her further in establishing Jonathan's identity.

Nor was she to be proved wrong. "I thought I could pay another visit to Brayton Manor and try and see Sir Henry's man, I believe he is called Kimble. He would be bound to know the details." Cressidia seemed pleased with her idea.

Sapphira, forestalling her twin's effort to disabuse Cressidia's mind of this belief, said with a puzzled frown wrinkling her brow, "But why should Sir Henry's valet know any more on the subject than Mrs Glossop?"

"Mama always said that papa's man knew more of his secrets than she did," Cressidia answered with aplomb.

This was obviously a clincher to the argument, for both sisters accepted the statement with no further demur. On reflection, Justin found himself in agreement with the late viscountess.

"It is not possible for you to pay yet another visit to the manor," Karenza said decidedly. "Not only does Mr Faversham probably suspect your motives, but also it would be quite shocking of you to impose yourself further on a household where the master is seriously ill, perhaps dying."

A mulish expression crossed Cressidia's face at these words, but wisely she did not seek to change her sister's mind, contenting herself instead with the contemplation of a variety of plans whereby she could gain access to Kimble without appearing odiously unfeeling.

Datchett's voice at the door informing them that his lordship's visitor had departed and asking if Miss Karenza wished to delay dinner any longer since it was already past six o'clock reminded his hearers that they had not yet changed. Karenza paused only to inform their servitor that it would be necessary to delay the meal another half hour and to beg him to soothe cook's ruffled feelings over their apparent neglect of her culinary efforts.

"Shall I acquaint his lordship with your wishes as well, Miss Karenza?" said Datchett rather pointedly, thus causing her to recall the viscount's earlier admonitions and reviving her resentment of them.

"Yes, and also ask Mr Jonathan to join us." Then nodding her dismissal, Karenza ran lightly up the stairs to her bedchamber.

When the group reassembled at the dining table, Justin lost little time in acquainting his uncle with the events of the afternoon, causing Cressidia to blush at his extravagant words of praise for her daring, while Jonathan, whose eyes fairly sparkled at the news, was soon entertaining them all with his suggestions of the family traits which promised to endear him to his grandfather. Everyone was by now making the not unnatural assumption that Jonathan was indeed the son of Sylvester Faversham.

"Perhaps it is the way I can twitch my ears or cross my eyes that is a family characteristic." With this, Jonathan gave a hideous example of both, to the amusement of his onlookers; even Darnborough was laughing, which enabled Karenza to address him in a relatively amicable manner.

"It is all very well to make fun of the matter, but we need to establish the facts without indulging in any foolish activity which would bring one in direct confrontation with

Beau Faversham." She glanced meaningfully at Cressidia as she spoke.

The viscount, shrewdly aware of what troubled his lovely ward, spoke with calm assurance. "There is no need to trouble yourself on that score, for I have the matter in hand."

"What do you mean to do?" There was relief and trust in her voice as Karenza gazed at him.

"Tomorrow I shall send a messenger to London with detailed instructions for Mr Ponsonby and a personal letter for Lady Wainforth. The former will request of Lady Wainforth her knowledge of the name and whereabouts of Sylvester's lawyer, from whom he would be able to gain the details we seek should Lady Wainforth be unable to supply them herself."

"Why, that's a splendid idea!" exclaimed Sapphira, while Justin cast his uncle an admiring glance.

"Well, I am sure that I wish your plan every success," said Karenza slowly, "but I have a feeling that it will take time to achieve—and that may not be granted to us. Beau Faversham is too intelligent not to realise the need to act quickly now that he knows Jonathan is with us."

"Whilst you may be right regarding the Beau's intentions, I fear it is the only way of legally establishing Jonathan's credentials until he regains his memory, and therefore we can only be on our guard against any further incursions in search of him." Darnborough's tone was serious, and the look he cast that young man showed only sympathetic understanding.

"Don't imagine that I am not grateful to you all," Jonathan said, all trace of banter gone from his voice. "But I can't help thinking I should be doing more to help myself. If I went to see Sir Henry, he might recognise me if I am so like my father."

"Good God, no! Have you broken loose from bedlam? Only a madman would take such a risk!" Justin's words reflected the thoughts of more than one of them at the table.

Cressidia's face whitened at the danger her beloved would encounter should he come face to face with the Beau. "Oh, pray, do not take any unnecessary risks; have patience and await the results of Cousin Darnborough's enquiry," she urged.

"And make sure you do likewise, Cressidia," his lordship added forbiddingly.

For a moment there was silence at the table; then Miss Brinton brought matters back to a lighter plane by a gentle enquiry as to whether or not the viscount would be prepared to receive visits from his neighbours, for it could not be supposed that they would be neglectful of extending such courtesies.

"Am I to understand, ma'am, that there are likely to be many such visits?" asked the viscount, looking rather dismayed at the prospect.

"Naturally!" said Miss Brinton in reproachful tones. "It would be very remiss of them to ignore such civilities. It would not, indeed, be proper to hold any parties whilst the family remain in black gloves, but one or two quiet dinners would not be adversely remarked upon."

The discussion then moved to those who would be expecting such invitations. Karenza silently debated whether or not to point out that the absence of she or Sapphira as hostess would limit these events by excluding the presence of any ladies. Deciding that this would probably be welcomed by her cousin, she promptly volunteered the information that she would be happy to preside at these festivities.

Such contrariness did not go unnoticed by her guardian, but he forbore from commenting on the fact until after dinner. Abandoning the remainder of the family to a noisy game of jackstraws under the benign gaze of Miss Brinton, his lordship seated himself next to Karenza on the small sofa at the far end of the saloon. Here he solemnly thanked her for sacrificing her principles in order for him to establish himself credibly with his neighbours.

She was much amused and replied with a mischievous look, "You must understand that it is for the benefit of our acquaintances, many of whom are our good friends, and I would not wish to give them cause for complaint."

"How very kind!" he approved with a glint of laughter in the grey eyes. "They would no doubt feel deeply obligated to you were they aware of your self-immolation on their behalf!"

"Now you are being absurd!" She gave a small chuckle, then abandoning her laughter, she said seriously, "Do you believe that Jonathan will be able to establish himself without regaining his memory?"

"That, cousin, is something I cannot tell, but I am persuaded that there is a strong likelihood that it can be achieved." He paused before adding with a cool certainty which was oddly comforting, "I do not intend to fail you in this matter."

Karenza glanced at him reflectively, but Darnborough, rising to his feet, added in a lighter tone, "You must excuse me if I leave you now, for I wish to write the letters I mentioned earlier. My man will leave at dawn with them and should thus be in London before darkness falls. The sooner he is off the better." He was spared the necessity of saying anything more by Cressidia demanding that her sister join them in a game of Speculation, and within moments the viscount had left the room and was not seen again before the rest of the family retired for the night.

The sense of unease that had been with her since the encounter with Beau Faversham remained with Karenza, so it was some time before she was able to find sleep—and even then she was restless, tossing and turning constantly.

She was not sure what it was that woke her, and for a moment she lay gazing at the ceiling above the open window, watching the patterns of shadow twist and flicker as clouds chased their way across the moon. There was something about them that drew her attention, and the gradual realisation that a pinkish glow was illuminating her room brought her suddenly from her bed.

Hastening to the window, her horrified gaze fastened on the sight of billowing smoke and flames coming from the direction of the stables. In the quiet night air she heard the frightened neighing of horses as they sought to escape.

Subconsciously remembering her guardian's order, Karenza pulled the bellcord urgently, at the same time hastily donning a minimum of clothing. She was already at the doorway and calling for her sisters as Datchett appeared, his nightcap still on his head and enveloped in a crimson dressing gown, which made him look more portly than ever.

"Miss Karenza, you're all right," he said with undisguised relief, panting from the exertion of climbing the stairs so quickly.

Swiftly, Karenza snapped out her orders as her sisters appeared on the scene. "Tell Lord Darnborough that the stables are on fire! Rouse the household and send all the men immediately to the stables. Hurry!" Suddenly she remembered Jonathan. For a moment she hesitated. But no, she could not put his life at risk. Already she had the uneasy feeling that this was no ordinary fire, and the suspicion that it had been started to get Jonathan out there in the darkness filled her mind. Much as she needed his care with the horses, he must stay in the house.

"Wait, Datchett! Urge Mr Jonathan to stay in the house. He will be in too much danger outside. Now go quickly!" She turned to her sisters, ignoring their exclamations of horror and the questions they threw at her. "Cressy! You and Sapphira take Jonathan to the music room and stay with him there. You go, too, Brinny dear. He will be safe with you. Pray, do not argue. I must go now—just do as I say, I beg of you!" Then she was gone, feet flying down the stairs and out the side door to gain the stables.

Foremost in her mind now was Buccaneer. "Oh God, please let him be all right!" she prayed frantically as she plunged through the smoke and felt the heat of the flames dancing near her face. There was no hesitation in her movements, nor did she check at sight of the devouring blaze. Now she was at the entrance to the great stallion's stable; her hands fumbled at the bolt as she called his name over and over again, trying to calm him as he lunged frantically against the open door.

At last the bolts slid free, and she flung herself aside as she pulled open the door just in time to miss the great hurtling body as it crashed its way to freedom and away from the terror of the flames. She made no effort to stop Buccaneer, thankful merely to see him fleeing, apparently unharmed, through the clouds of smoke. Tomorrow she would go looking for him. He would not travel far once he felt out of danger.

Now she was at the other stables but no longer alone. Beside her Mr Drover came to her aid, and without speaking they hurled themselves at door after stable door amidst the wild squealings of frightened animals.

The horses were all free now, but there was still the clash of hooves on cobblestones as some sought but failed to find the path away from the heat and the smoke. A terrible tiredness came upon her, and her head felt dizzy with the effects of the fumes. She swayed on her feet. Strong, comforting arms wrapped themselves around her, and the next moment the viscount swept her off her feet and carried her with enormous gentleness away from the smells and fumes of burning timbers and straw. Tears of relief poured down her face which she was helpless to control. His arms around her tightened their grip, and he murmured comforting messages, reassuring her over and over again that all was well.

"Jonathan. Is Jonathan safe?" The grip encompassing her tightened, then the viscount's voice came through the swirling mist that was filling her brain, telling her that her beloved was in no danger, was still in the house, protected by her sisters.

She wanted to answer, to say that he was not her beloved but Cressidia's, but it was too much of an effort; the mist became thicker and thicker as she slipped deeper into unconsciousness. The viscount carried his burden with tender care into the house and up into the bedchamber, where he stood for a moment gazing, almost with anguish, into her pale, lovely face before ordering, in an expressionless voice, one of the grooms to take an urgent demand for Doctor Beech to present himself once more at the Hall.

14

It was well into the morning before Karenza finally regained her senses and opened her eyes to find the doctor's familiar face smiling down at her. Aware of a tightness in her chest and a throbbing behind her eyes, she regarded him with some perplexity as she sought to account for her woes. Then his words brought memories flooding back.

"You'll soon be right as ninepence, Miss Karenza. 'Twas the inhalation of all that smoke that's caused your trouble. Just take the day quietly, and by tomorrow you'll be feeling yourself again. You are already better than when I saw you last night. Now I best be off to reassure his lordship, for I warrant he is more than anxious to hear how you go on."

Karenza shot up in her bed. "Buccaneer!" she gasped. "I must find Buccaneer!"

Sapphira pushed her sister gently back onto her pillows. "The creature is quite safe," she said soothingly. "Mr Drover found him and brought him back soon after the fire was brought under control. Jonathan assures me that he has come to no harm. Now stop being a pea-goose, and do as Doctor Beech has said."

The doctor closed his case and cast his patient a keen look from under his bushy brows. "There'll be bellows to mend with you, Miss Karenza, if you try to go riding today. Now

173

you be a good girl and do as I say. You'll not be wanting much to eat, perhaps a little thin gruel could be attempted, but try to drink the cordial I will send to you. Now I best go, or my other patients will think I have taken up residence at Darnborough Hall!"

When the doctor had gone, Karenza turned a worried face to her twin. "It was Mr Drover who helped me free the horse; I remember now how he suddenly appeared beside me. Why was he there? Did he see Jonathan?"

"Jonathan stayed with Cressy and me, though he was much loath to do so. When Cousin Darnborough returned with you in his arms and said what had happened, Jonathan wanted to leave at once to find Buccaneer, but our cousin regarded him most oddly and said that he would tie Jonathan to a chair next to you if he made any attempt to leave the house." Sapphira shook her head in bewilderment. "Why should he want to leave Jonathan with you? Especially at such a time! Really, his behaviour was most peculiar."

"Well, I am glad he kept Jonathan from going outside, for I am certain that the fire was started for the purpose of luring him into the open," Karenza said, pushing back the bedclothes.

"Karenza! You cannot be getting up; you heard what dear Doctor Beech recommended. Do not disregard—"

"There is nothing really wrong with me and much for me to do," Karenza said, breaking in on her sister's agitation. "I must find Cousin Darnborough, for there is a lot I wish to know. Do help me with my dressing; if I send for Jenny, she will fuss and fluster beyond all bearing."

As she spoke, there was a soft tap at the door and Cressidia's anxious face peered round it. She broke into a relieved smile as she saw her eldest sister looking at her enquiringly. "Oh, I'm so glad you are recovered!" she said, dancing up to her and embracing her warmly. "The whole house has been at sixes and sevens from the moment you were brought back by our cousin, and poor Brinny has had such a task convincing the servants that you were not about to die and trying to cope with the numerous callers and offers of help that have been pouring in since first light this morning," she ended breathlessly.

"Good God, Cressy!" Karenza exclaimed, hastily completing her toilet. "I trust our visitors have now dispersed."

"Most of them, but when dear Brinny tried to encourage Sir James to leave, he took offence, said that he trusted that we did not expect him to run sly in your hour of need and looked most reproachful."

"Well, of all the addle-pated creatures! As though he could do anything for us! Why didn't Darnborough get rid of him?" Karenza said crossly.

"Perhaps he thinks that you are more than a little fond of Sir James," Sapphira suggested, looking whimsically at her twin.

"Then he's got more wit than hair if he thinks that. Anyway, I've no wish to meet Sir James, for we should only end by quarreling. Where is he now?"

"You are quite safe," Cressidia assured her. "Justin suggested that Sir James might assist him in riding in search of the two horses that are still missing. They are trying to follow their tracks before they disappear."

Looking relieved at this information, and brushing aside her sisters' remonstrances, Karenza made her way down the stairs and through the hallway to the main saloon to find his lordship, who was on the point of departing to inspect the damage done to the stables.

As he heard their footsteps he turned round, and a warm smile lit the usually stern features. "My dear girl, are you sure you should be up and about?" he asked, coming towards her and taking her hands in his. There was no mistaking his pleasure at the sight of her, and Karenza found herself responding to the warmth of his greeting with an unusually friendly smile.

"I assure you that I am fully recovered. Doctor Beech is something of a fusspot, dear creature that he is. Now, if you can but spare me a moment, I would like to know how things go on."

"You certainly have every right to know. But for your fortunate discovery of the fire, matters could have been more serious than they are. Please, come and sit down."

When the three young ladies were comfortably disposed, the viscount took a turn or two about the room before saying, with an usually serious note in his voice, "It is my opinion that the fire was started deliberately, and Ben Drover, who appeared so fortuitously upon the scene, agrees with me."

"I was most glad to have his help," Karenza exclaimed, "but what was his purpose being there at such a late hour?"

Darnborough twirled his quizzing glass thoughtfully before replying. "I fear that he still suspects us of hiding the infamous Dan Gunn and was keeping watch on the premises."

"He must be a sapskull to think that Jonathan could be the one he seeks!" Cressidia said with asperity.

"Did I hear my name mentioned?" a laughing voice interposed as Jonathan came into the room. "I'm devilishly glad to see you are well again, Karenza," he said feelingly. "Lord! What a fright we had last night when Darnborough brought you back unconscious! You put us all to shame with your courage. I can tell you it went against the pluck for me to remain in the house when your cousins and the menservants went off to deal with the fire. I nearly came to fisticuffs with Darnborough over it."

"Well, I'm very glad that you didn't," Karenza replied, smiling up into the indignant young face.

"Oh well, I daresay he would have landed me a facer if we had done so," Jonathan said with admirable frankness. His lordship, running his eyes over the muscular young man, gave his opinion that he had no doubt that Jonathan was a devil with his fives himself and probably frequented Jackson's when in town.

Such sporting talk was of little interest to the ladies, and Karenza quickly interrupted to ask anxiously of Jonathan if Buccaneer had taken any hurt the previous night.

On hearing that her equine friend had suffered no more than a fright and was now contentedly grazing in the field near the orchard, she was able to relax. After a warning to him to make sure there were no fallen apples available— for Buccaneer had a great weakness for them and too many would give him the colic—she was able to turn her attention back to the events of the previous night.

"You were saying, cousin, that the fire had been started deliberately. Did you find any trace of those responsible for such a dastardly act?" she asked.

"I fear not, though I sensed that the perpetrator was near to the scene, and more than once I thought I saw a shadowy figure lurking nearby. Drover went after him, but without success. It was easy to hide in the darkness and the smoke, as well as all the confusion, as men tackled the fire. But I could swear that he was searching for something or someone."

All further discussion on the matter halted at the sudden sound of voices in the hallway.

The next moment the door was flung open to reveal a somewhat harassed-looking Justin, still in his riding clothes. "Mama's here!" he announced in a voice which held a mixture of pleasure and apprehension. Beyond him, in the entrance hall, could be seen two females, one of whom was issuing a stream of instructions on the disposal of her luggage to a bemused Datchett and her agitated abigail.

No sooner had he spoken than Lady Mapping swept through the open doorway, her hands outstretched in greeting to her brother, who came forward to meet her.

"My dear Georgie, I had no doubt that you would be wishing to see for yourself that Justin was in no danger of sticking his spoon to the wall, but you should have sent us word when to expect you."

"Nonsense, dear brother! You should have known that I would come as soon as I got your letter. No mother would rest content at home after such news. I left the very next day, and my dearest Frederick was only too sorry that estate matters prevented him from accompanying me." Giving him no time to reply to these words, Lady Mapping turned to where the three young ladies stood together, regarding her a trifle uncertainly.

"My dears, I shall stand on no formality with you. I am delighted to meet with you at last. Now tell me, for I cannot see any difference 'twixt the two of you, which one is Karenza and which Sapphira?"

It was not hard for Karenza to respond to such a friendly approach. She said smilingly, "I am Karenza, ma'am, and this is Sapphira; we are constantly mistaken for each other."

"We are most happy to have you with us, ma'am," Sapphira said shyly, while Justin came forward to hover protectively at her side. Lady Mapping glanced at them shrewdly, but made no comment as she turned to greet the third young lady.

"I am the middle one, ma'am, Cressidia, or Cressy as the family like to call me," Cressidia said with considerable aplomb as she made her curtsey.

"Then I hope you will consider me a member of the family and allow me to also address you as Cressy. What lovely names you all have. 'Karenza' is one I've not heard before," Lady Mapping remarked with interest.

"It is an old Cornish name, ma'am. I was called after my great-grandmother, whose family came from that part of the world," Karenza explained. "But allow me to introduce you to a very special guest," she said, drawing Jonathan forward and at the same time wondering by what name to present him.

She need not have worried. "Oh, there is no need to do that," said Lady Mapping blithely. "How are you, my dear Jonathan? You deserve that I should give you a good scolding for calling on me only once since your return to England."

There was a stunned silence, the company totally at a loss for words as they gazed in disbelief at the speaker.

"You mean that you know this young man, Georgina?" the viscount asked in tones of utter incredulity.

"Of course I do, Marcus. It should cause you no surprise. I was at school with his dear mama—he is, in fact, my godson!"

"Your godson!" echoed Cressidia in a dazed manner.

"Then you'll be aware of his full name," Darnborough said reflectively.

"Well naturally I know it. I was at the christening. Really, Marcus, you are being positively dull-witted!"

"Pray, humour me, dear sister, and inform us of your godson's appellations."

She gave an uncomprehending shrug before saying, "I don't know why you must make such a fuss about it; surely he could tell you himself. Still, if you must have my word for it, he was christened Jonathan James Henry and his surname, of course, is Faversham."

There was total silence in the great saloon. Then Jonathan put his arms round his godmother and bestowed on each cheek a fervent kiss.

"Ma'am," he said gratefully, "you are indeed my fairy godmother!"

"Well, bless the boy. I did not quite expect such a greeting!" She paused and looked at the little group, her grey eyes dancing with amusement. "I think you have something to tell me."

"Indeed, we have, Lady Mapping. But first let me escort you to your room. You must be tired from your long journey and in need of refreshment," Sapphira said with gentle concern.

"Oh, I'm not at all tired, although the journey was a trifle tedious. I spent the night with some dear friends, who reside less than fifteen miles away. You probably know them, General Sir Michael and Lady Finch-Melchett." As she spoke, Lady Mapping unbuttoned her pelisse and abandoned her modish hat on a chair. She moved over to the sofa where Karenza had seated herself and sat down beside her. "I can restrain my curiosity no longer. Do tell me why you were all so interested in the fact that I knew Jonathan."

"Well, it all began when Sapphira and I found Jonathan in the woods," said Cressidia, electing herself as spokesman and immediately launching forth into a detailed account of all that had happened, while his lordship lounged back in his chair to watch his sister's reactions with something akin to resignation.

As Cressidia completed her saga, Lady Mapping turned to her son. "And to think that I was imagining you rusticating in the tranquillity of the countryside!" she exclaimed.

Before she had time to develop this theme, Karenza, after a swift look at Jonathan, earnestly requested dear Lady

Mapping to enlighten them on the subject of Jonathan's family background.

"Yes, for lord's sake, satisfy our curiosity, Georgie," interposed his lordship. "When I think of all the efforts that have gone into trying to establish Jonathan's identity when all the time my own sister held the key to the whole problem, I feel decidedly blue-deviled."

"Then I won't keep you in suspense, for it must be particularly hard for Jonathan in these circumstances." She leant forward and gave his hand a sympathetic pat before continuing in a brisker tone. "Eliza Standish and I were pupils together at Miss Frobisher's seminary in Bath. Eliza's father, Samuel, was a wealthy merchant who spent most of his time in India, although he had a house in London, in Russell Square, though he was seldom there. I suppose he sent her to the school—and I've no doubt he paid an excessive price for the privilege—because he was anxious for his daughter to mix with the ton. She was his only child and he wanted her to marry well; besides which, the Indian climate was not suitable for a young girl."

"What about Eliza's mother?" Cressidia asked anxiously.

"She died shortly after Eliza was born, and the baby was reared by a maiden aunt. Eliza saw her father at intervals when he came to England."

"Oh, the poor little soul!" exclaimed Sapphira, her heart touched by the plight of the motherless child.

"Anyway, Eliza and I became bosom-bows and swore eternal friendship; even after leaving school we still occasionally wrote to each other. Then her aunt died and Eliza decided to visit her father in Bombay. By then she was about twenty-two and still unattached. She met Sylvester on the boat out. I believe Sylvester had fought a duel and had to leave the country rather suddenly. They fell in love and married shortly after their arrival in India. Sir Henry was furious and promptly disowned his son, but Samuel Frobisher took Sylvester into partnership and they dealt extremely well together. Five years later, Samuel died of a fever and Sylvester brought Eliza back to England. They came to stay with Frederick and me before buying a small estate in Hertfordshire on the outskirts of St Albans, and it was there that Jonathan was born." She glanced at Jonathan who was watching her with painful intensity. "You were a lovely baby, and they were so proud of you and happy together. I remember your christening in Sandridge church and the celebration afterwards at the Heath, which is the name of your parents' residence. I suppose it is yours now. Anyway, they lived there very happily for the next six years; there were no more children. Their life was fairly quiet, they did not go much into Society. Sir Henry would still have nothing to do with them, although I think he was beginning to regret it, but was too proud to admit he had been wrong."

Jonathan gave a grimace. "He does not sound the type of man to win one's affection."

"I think he has been perfectly horrid!" said Cressidia indignantly. "But what happened when Jonathan was six?"

"Sadly, Eliza died. Sylvester was heartbroken. He let the Heath to a tenant and returned to India with Jonathan. Later he sent Jonathan to school in England. After that we tended to lose touch with each other. I rather gather that Sylvester appointed an old school friend as his guardian, and Jonathan spent most of his holidays with his guardian's family. I believe Sylvester's aunt, Lady Wainforth, did offer to have him, but for some reason or another that came to nothing. Anyway, when he was eighteen, he joined his father in India and remained with him until Sylvester's death a year ago. As soon as he had wound up the not-inconsiderable business, he returned to England. I suppose, Jonathan, you must have got back about six months ago. That was when you came to see me. You were intending to visit your parents' Hertfordshire estate once you had sorted out the legal matters with your lawyer. And that is about all I can tell you."

"Thank you so very much indeed, dear ma'am!" Jonathan said gratefully. "It is such a comfort to me to have at least one person who can guarantee my identity."

"My compliments for your admirably succinct account, Georgie." His lordship looked at his sister approvingly. "Yet, I fear that Jonathan will still need to produce documentary evidence to support his claim to be Sir Henry's grandson."

Karenza turned to him with a worried expression. "This delay can only provide Beau Faversham, if he is indeed the one who seeks Jonathan's life—and I am sure that he is—more time to dispose of his rival."

The viscount took a delicate pinch of snuff and inhaled it gently before saying in an expressionless tone, "He would be safer away from this district."

"Oh no!" exclaimed Karenza, horrified at this threat to her plans.

The viscount gazed upon his ward with an unfathomable look on his face. "Now, I wonder why you should object to my suggestion?"

"Will you have the goodness to permit me to make the decision for myself?" interrupted Jonathan, in a half-humorous tone. "If you are prepared to continue to have me as a guest in your house, I would as lief remain here. For all the wrong he has done my parents, Sir Henry is still my grandfather, and I should like to see him before he dies; in which case it is better to remain not too distant from him. Another reason is that . . . well . . ." Here he hesitated as though not sure how to go on, before adding awkwardly,

"I do not wish to go, as I should be amongst strangers. Here I feel I am with friends whom I know and whom I hold in great affection. I would loath to leave you, unless you wish me to," he ended, and none of his listeners could fail to be touched by the pathos of these words as he cast them an appealing look.

"Of course you shall stay with us." There were tears in Cressidia's eyes as she spoke for them all. "Cousin Darnborough would not be so cruel as to send you away," she stated positively, throwing her guardian a reproachful look.

"Pray, do not cast me in the role of a monster, since all I seek is Jonathan's safety and to protect my wards' well-being," the viscount said in exasperated tones.

"Well then, now that that is settled," Lady Mapping said affably, "I will ask my dear Justin to take me for a short perambulation in the garden. We had little time to talk when he met my chaise less than a mile from the Hall, and there is much I wish to tell him about his brothers and sisters. If you will excuse us for a brief while." Then with a sweet smile she placed a hand on Justin's arm, and together they left the room, leaving Lord Darnborough gazing thoughtfully after them.

It was not long before the remaining company were scattered—the viscount to complete his tour of the stables and Sapphira to organise the household to cope with their additional guest and to ensure that fresh flowers were placed in Lady Mapping's room. Seizing the opportunity, Karenza withdrew to the sofa by the window to ponder once again her racing instructions, while Jonathan and Cressidia departed to inform Miss Brinton of the latest developments in the Faversham saga.

Returning from the stables for a light luncheon, his lordship was peremptorily hailed by his sister as she stood alone in the garden, near the side entrance.

"Justin has informed me that he intends to marry Sapphira and will do so with or without your consent!" she exclaimed dramatically.

"Since they both come of age within a few months, my consent will make little difference," her brother said discouragingly. "Still, if you do not wish to be alienated from your son, I should, if I were you, accept the marriage with compliance. He could do worse for himself."

"I must admit I am favourably impressed with Sapphira and Karenza. They seem modest, well-brought-up girls; they are certainly very lovely."

"Oh yes, diamonds of the first water," Darnborough agreed affably.

"What is their fortune? I do not want to sound at all grasping, but naturally one wishes for one's son to marry a person who can bring a reasonable settlement to the marriage."

His lordship frowned slightly. "Their means are very modest. But never fear. I will ensure that each of my wards shall be properly endowed on marriage. I knew it would be so when I first heard of my inheritance. It is fortunate," he said a little wryly, "that they have a wealthy man for their guardian, when you think there are five of them! Still, never fear, I shall do my duty by them!"

It was unfortunate that Lady Mapping should seek to reassure Karenza, during the cosiest of talks after leaving her brother, that the viscount was not only favourably disposed towards the proposed marriage between Sapphira and her darling Justin—and here Lady Mapping paused to say in a kindly tone that she had quite lost her heart to Sapphira and was looking forward to welcoming her as a daughter— but was also prepared to make a generous marriage settlement on Sapphira's behalf. Was he not, indeed, a most caring guardian; how fortunate they were to be in the charge of one who was willing to bestow such patronage upon them.

Poor lady! Did she but know her words were as wormwood and gall to a proud Karenza, who bitterly resented the assumption that she would be only too glad to be the recipient of Lord Darnborough's charity.

Furious thoughts filled that young lady's mind. Cressidia would have no need of a London Season, not now that her future with Jonathan seemed more or less secure. Any winnings from Buccaneer's race could and should be spent on providing Sapphira with her bridal array as well as a small dowry that would owe nothing to the patronage of the sixth viscount. Five thousand pounds could be hers to lovingly bestow on her sister. Thus it was with renewed determination that Karenza turned her mind to consider her tactics for the great race, now only two days away, while Lady Mapping continued to extol the virtues of her dear brother into decidedly unreceptive ears.

15

It was felt that, although still in mourning, it would not come amiss for the Darnborough family to accept Sir Peter's kind invitation to attend the private race meeting at Buckley Manor. For, as Karenza had been swift to point out, Sir Peter had been one of her father's closest friends and would no doubt wish to use this occasion to pay a tribute to the man who had shared his passion for the turf. As the invitation to the sixth viscount included any house guests he would care to bring, Lady Mapping and Justin were amongst the apparently relaxed and cheerful party that prepared to leave the Hall that morning. Thus it was that the three elder Misses Coningsby, together with Lady Mapping, decorously took their places in the landaulet, while the gentlemen on horseback fell in behind the carriage.

Telling the coachman to make a start, Karenza cast a significant look at Jonathan as he raised a hand in farewell. He had made surprisingly little demur when informed by his lordship that he must remain out of sight at the Hall during their absence. His response made the viscount regard him with a sense of unease and determine to keep Karenza under close observation that day.

Sapphira's habitual quiet this time masked her dread of the role she was to play that afternoon. She was not a natural conspirator, and she felt a sense of anguish at deceiving her dearest Justin. Indeed, it was only that special bond that tied her to her twin that enabled her to contemplate undertaking the action that her more daring sister demanded of her. For Sapphira was to spend the afternoon flitting from one group to another, one minute herself, another impersonating Karenza. Only those who knew them very well could distinguish between the two, and those Sapphira would be careful to avoid. It was vital, her twin impressed upon her, that the viscount should be amongst those deceived. Indeed, no one should have cause to associate her with the riders in the great race. Karenza was only too aware of the shocked horror with which Society would view her escapade should it become known.

Her instructions had been clear. On arrival, they would meet their host, as expected of them. Karenza had already informed Sir Peter that she was entering Buccaneer in the race, as her father would have wished her to do so, and without exactly giving a reason, had somehow impressed on him the need to keep it as a surprise for the new viscount. They would mingle with their friends until fifteen minutes before the great race, when both were to make their separate ways to the prearranged spot in the woods where Jonathan would be awaiting them with Buccaneer. There, Karenza would don the rest of her riding outfit, and Sapphira would return to the manor taking her sister's pelisse to wear during her impersonation of her twin. Near the end of the race, Sapphira was to make her way to the point where Jonathan would take Karenza's place as Buccaneer's rider and ride back to receive the winner's plaudits (or so they hoped), while Karenza would don her pelisse and bonnet. Then the two sisters would rejoin their friends.

For this reason, Karenza's ensemble had been carefully chosen to include—as distinctive from her twin's grey with black trimmings—a deep lavender pelisse which buttoned up to hide the buckskin breeches and the shirt, with its fresh white neckcloth, that she wore beneath it. An old portmanteau containing the accompanying coat of black Bath suiting, shining boots with snowy tops and a curly brimmed beaver hat—all part of a gentleman's riding outfit—having been carefully hidden the previous day in the copse where Karenza had arranged to meet Jonathan with Buccaneer. Karenza had considered cutting her hair in the new shorter fashion, but vigorous protests from Sapphira, who balked at this sacrifice, persuaded her to agree they should both wear their locks twisted in a knot atop their heads that would be hidden by their poke bonnets and later, so far as Karenza was concerned, by a firmly pinned beaver riding hat. Identical reticules and gloves in black—brighter colours being out of the question since they were still in mourning—were not forgotten.

Jonathan would be wearing riding apparel similar to that of Karenza's—both outfits having been provided by an obliging, if somewhat puzzled, tailor in Huntingdon at Karenza's written request. If their fit was not one that would meet with the approval of Mr Weston or Mr Schultz, it nevertheless fulfilled their purpose. Karenza could only be glad that the riders were confined to owners and their friends, mostly the young bloods of the district, and not the more plebeian jockeys, who would have been quick to penetrate any disguise.

Karenza was beginning to feel more than a little nervous as the moment of action approached, but she kept it well hidden. It had not been difficult to detach herself from her guardian and his relations, and she was pleased to note that Sapphira had done likewise. As she paused to chat with old friends, enjoying the opportunity to take part once more in the social life of the Huntingdonshire ton—something she had missed since the death of her father—she still ensured that her direction took her slowly towards the point at which she was to meet Jonathan.

Keeping an air of nonchalance, Karenza finally drifted away from the crowd and made her way to the wooded copse where she had arranged to meet her co-conspirators, all the time carefully watching to see if anyone, other than Sapphira, had marked her going. Then, certain she had not been observed, she slipped quietly through the trees to retrieve her portmanteau and don her riding clothes with urgent fingers.

"For God's sake, let me ride Buccaneer! There'll be a deuce of a kick-up if you're discovered." Jonathan made a final desperate plea as he reluctantly assisted Karenza to mount the great horse, while a trembling Sapphira added her voice to his.

Karenza shook her head. "Let's not waste time in arguing; just remember what you must do," she said curtly, irritated by the assumption that she was likely to change her mind at this late stage. She softened her words with a farewell smile as she put her feet in the stirrups. Then dismissing everything from her mind except what lay ahead of her, she walked her horse free of the trees and in the direction of the starting line.

Buccaneer was in a killing mood. Karenza could feel his anger flowing through him. He had these moods from time to time. Mentally she rebuked him, letting him know that there was no time for tantrums, that he had to win. The telepathy between the horse and her had always been there; it was why she knew that she was the only one who could channel his energy and speed to win the race. All the way along the winding track to the starting point the contest of wills went on unabated.

There were fourteen horses awaiting the start of the race, many resenting the tedium of the delay and showing it in their kicking and bucking, so that Karenza had good reason to keep out of the way and stayed well to the rear.

They got off to a slow start, Buccaneer expressing his anger by doggedly refusing to increase his pace. Karenza knew she could only keep urging him on until he worked himself out of his bad mood and trust it would not occur too late. It was not long before a feeling of despair filled her as Buccaneer sulkily trailed the field; they were a hundred yards behind now, and already the race was half over.

Then suddenly, as though he sensed his rider's feelings and felt ashamed of himself, Buccaneer's pace altered. The bad temper left him, and he surged forward yard by yard, flying past his competitors. The great stallion galloped with fearsome, indomitable strides, going ever faster, passing horse after horse, until only Sir Peter's pride and joy, Ulysses, lay ahead of him. Karenza automatically crouched lower till almost flat along the line of his neck, telling him how wonderful he was and urging him ever onward. Ulysses was tiring now on the final uphill stretch, and a smugly triumphant Buccaneer swept past him, a bare few feet from the winning post! A loud chorus of cheers from the onlookers greeted the exciting and popular victory.

Karenza made no attempt to check Buccaneer's speed, but carried on towards the wooded area over the brow of the hill, making a great pretence of trying to pull the horse up, though to no avail, thus giving the impression of it being out of control to all but one mounted spectator, who spurred his horse in hot pursuit.

Once out of sight, she sought to check the speed of their approach as they entered the woodland path, ducking suddenly to miss a low-hanging branch. At the same moment, the explosion from a gun behind them caused Buccaneer to swerve violently, and Karenza, already off balance, was thrown to the ground, losing consciousness as her head met the hard upthrust of a tree root. She did not hear the sound of the second shot and the dying scream that followed it nor the peculiarly sweet yet shrill whistle from Jonathan that arrested the headlong flight of the riderless horse as it came upon him through the trees.

It was the surprising sight of Ben Drover leaning over Karenza's still figure that brought a gasp of horror to Jonathan's lips, as still grasping the reins of the sweating, snorting stallion, he came out onto the path.

"What have you done to her, you devil!" he called in anguish, letting go of Buccaneer, who seemed happy to stand, his head down and his great sides heaving as he regained his breath.

"Mum your dubber, Mr Nib-Cove! This gentry-mort ain't got no bullet in her," Drover said tersely, scanning Jonathan's face with hard, shrewd eyes before adding phlegmatically, "Not that she won't have a lump the size of my fist on her head when she comes to her senses, or my name ain't Ben Drover—and yours ain't Dan Gunn, either, more's the pity," he added in a more resigned tone, "though I've yet to ken your lay, a pretty dance you've led me this day!"

Relieved yet disconcerted by these words, Jonathan dropped to his knees by Karenza's still form, but as he slipped a careful arm under her to raise her up, she gave a soft moan.

He was not the only one to hear Drover's comforting statement. Even as he sought to loosen her neckcloth, a familiar figure came from behind the trees and knelt at his side. If his lordship looked unnaturally pale, his voice retained its usual crisp authority.

"Leave Karenza to me, Jonathan. If you wish to save her good name, get yourself onto that animal and down to where Sir Peter is awaiting you. Sapphira is on her way here. I passed her at the bottom of the hill. Stop her and tell her to go back to my sister—and as herself, I hasten to add. Tell her to inform everyone that the excitement of seeing Buccaneer win the race appeared too much for Karenza after her recent accident at the fire, and that I have taken her home." He paused to look down at the boyish figure lying in his arms, a look of reluctant admiration mixed with understanding in his eyes. "Tell Sapphira to collect the prize on behalf of her sister. Now go. Lest others come to search for Buccaneer and his rider."

The unnatural silence that greeted these words attracted the viscount's attention. He looked at Jonathan, who was staring at him, a conflict of expressions crossing his face.

"I am Jonathan Faversham. I am! I know I am!" The words burst from the young man's lips as his mind reeled under the impact of this revelation. "Someone did try to kill me, I remember it now! It was the sound of the pistol shot that brought it all back to me! I can recall everything!" There was no mistaking the joy in Jonathan's voice as he gazed at the two men in front of him.

"Aye, and there was one peevy-cull tried again, right here and now—only he made the mistake of thinking you was the rider of this great big brute, happened that he missed, which was fortunate-like for the young lady. Afore he could try any more of 'is tricks, I dropped him like a pigeon." Ben Drover gently slid his long-nosed pistol from his pocket and regarded it thoughtfully before returning it to its hiding place, while his listeners regarded him in astonishment.

"There is obviously more we must discuss, Mr Drover," his lordship said a trifle grimly. "But first things first. Jonathan, delay no more. Get going on that horse—it was lucky you were able to stop him. I would have expected the animal to be in the next county by now."

"Yes, well that's a family trait I've inherited, the ability to communicate thus with horses; never did think it would be quite so useful," he said absentmindedly, gazing down at Karenza, worried by her pallor. "Shall I ask for a carriage to be sent up here, my lord?" he added anxiously.

"No! We must attract no attention. As soon as I am satisfied that Karenza is well enough, I'll carry her back on my horse. He'll take the two of us easily enough, and we can go by the back ways. Now waste no more time, Jonathan! Leave us before anyone else comes."

With a last concerned glance at Karenza and a nod in the direction of Ben Drover, Jonathan leaped onto Buccaneer's back and gathered up the reins. He looked down on Darnborough. "I shall return as soon as possible to the Hall," he said briefly, before adding with a wry grin, "though some would no doubt say that bedlam would be a much more appropriate place for us!" Then pressing his heels to the horse's flanks, he moved briskly down the path and was soon lost from sight.

The viscount eased himself from his coat and made it into a soft pillow, then gently lifted Karenza's head to place it under her. As he did so, her eyelids fluttered open and she gazed up at him in puzzled bewilderment.

"You!" she exclaimed weakly. "What has happened? Oh dear, my head does hurt!"

"I'd be surprised if it didn't; you gave it a pretty hard knock when you fell off your horse," the viscount told her frankly, but the warm concern in his eyes belied the bluntness of his words. "Rest quietly. When you're feeling better I'll take you home," he added comfortingly.

Gratefully, Karenza closed her eyes and allowed herself to drift away in a haze of half-remembered thoughts and swirling mists of pain and nausea.

Darnborough rose to his feet and turned to see Ben Drover sitting patiently under a tree, cleaning his pistol. The sight of it reminded his lordship of what the runner had done. He walked slowly across to him and looked down into the man's hard brown eyes. Drover returned an unblinking stare.

"Mr Drover, I think I should see the man whom you shot. I could perhaps identify him for you," he said coolly.

Drover got to his feet. "Well, the same thought had crossed my mind. Follow me, my lord." Then without a backward glance, Drover led the way back down the path towards the bend. Here he hesitated a moment before plunging into the bushes on the right of the track. Within a few feet of it a body was sprawled, face down amongst the grass and leaves. Drover bent down and turned it gently over. Darnborough found himself gazing into the cold dead features of Beau Faversham.

There was a long silence. Darnborough remained staring at the dead man, while his mind worked furiously on how to avoid any scandal linking Karenza to this latest event. At last he raised his head to look at Drover.

The runner looked back at him. "Well, my lord?"

"Mr Drover," said Darnborough slowly, "I have a notion that it would serve neither of us if the truth of today's events were noised abroad."

The runner looked at him with an air of mild interest. "Now I wonders what puts such an idea into your lordship's head," he remarked thoughtfully.

"As you undoubtedly realise, I wish to avoid any scandal attached to my name," the viscount said bluntly. "But I am also sure that it would not be to your advantage to be accused of having killed Sir Henry Faversham's grandson, Percy Faversham, in mistake for a notorious highwayman."

There was a pregnant pause. Mr Drover's gaze shifted from the viscount's face back to the dead man. He pointed to the Beau's gun, which lay lay near where he had fallen. "He was after murdering the rider of that great black brute, Buccaneer I think you calls it. I was duty bound to stop him."

"That would be hard to prove without our support," the viscount reminded him gently. "Listen to me," he added coaxingly, "the truth will help neither of us. There are many who will declare that you exceeded your authority whatever we say, and Miss Coningsby's good name would also suffer."

"I know why you're so anxious to pitch a Canterbury tale, and you don't gammon me that it is out of any thought to save me from trouble. Still, it won't come amiss to hear the story you would like to put about, if I agreed with you, that is," Drover said, turning away from the body and moving back onto the path.

The viscount followed him until they were once more in sight of Karenza, who still lay unmoving except for the occasional turning of her head as she sought to relieve its aching pain.

"I'm obliged to you," said Darnborough lightly before continuing on a more serious note. "We leave here without saying anything. Eventually a search party will go out, and a hint or two will no doubt get them going in this direction, where they will find the Beau's body, with his pistol in his hand."

"God love you, that won't satisfy anybody! There needs to be a reason for his death!" said Drover explosively.

"The Beau was killed by Dan Gunn!" said Darnborough, ignoring the interruption. "It was Percy Faversham, was it not, who first informed you of a highwayman being in this area? In fact, he insisted he had been seen in the woods of my estate."

"Well, yes. It ain't queering anybody's pitch if I tells you that he was the Rum Ned who laid the information like," Drover admitted cautiously.

"There you have it, then. Gunn revenging himself on an informer is something everyone will understand, and being blamed for a murder he did not do will in no way alter Dan Gunn's fate, should the authorities ever catch him, since his offences are already a hanging matter."

"Where does that leave me, except as a blubber-headed flat in the eyes of them at headquarters?" growled Drover.

His lordship regarded him not unsympathetically. "You and I are both men of the world and know you'll get small thanks from your superiors if you involve them in attempting to justify your killing of a member of the ton with many powerful friends who won't believe his guilt. I understand your feelings, believe me, but if I have to choose between you and protecting my ward's good name, then I have no alternative but to refuse to support your story."

"Oh, I'm flash to what your nibs intends to do," said Drover bitterly, "and I have no option but to keep my chaffer close. You'd go into the witness box yourself and give your oath that that would-be sheep-biter was as innocent as a newborne babe."

"Mr Drover, I do what I have to do, but I do not forget that my ward owes her life to your actions. Believe me, it is not a thing I shall ever forget, and when you retire from your calling, there will always be a ready hand to help you at Darnborough Hall." There was no need to say more.

The two men regarded each other steadily. "Well, if that's the story we're going to tell, we best get away from here," said Drover with some violence.

A sudden thought struck Darnborough. "By the way, I had information from London today that Jonathan Faversham's lawyers have grown anxious at his nonappearance at Buckley Manor, and a handsome reward has been offered for information concerning his whereabouts. You should return to London immediately with the news they seek and claim the reward—a quite handsome amount, I believe. Had you not followed our young friend I have no doubt that the Beau would have killed him once he discovered his mistake over Miss Coningsby, so you more than deserve what is offered."

"Well, I'm with you in that," responded the runner. "And I won't accuse you of offering it to me as a bribe to back your story, 'cause I fancy that lord or no lord, you ain't so beef-brained as to treat me like some basket-scrambler."

"No, I certainly do not think that, Mr Drover. Indeed, it has been a privilege to have met you. I trust you will call on me next time you are in this neighbourhood." There was no mistaking the sincerity in the viscount's voice.

"Dang me if you ain't a great gun, my lord! 'Tis best, then, if I leave you now 'less you want my help with the young lady there?"

The viscount smilingly shook his head and watched in silence as the runner melted quietly into the trees and was soon lost to sight. Then he turned and made his way back to where Karenza lay watching him.

Once more he knelt beside his ward. "Are you feeling better now?" he asked gently.

Her hand came up to clasp his arm. "I remember now! We won! We really won the race!"

"Yes, you won!" Darnborough said as he looked down at her.

Grey eyes met green eyes. A message passed between them.

"You're not angry with me, then?" she asked confidently, feeling slightly breathless.

"You deserve to have your neck wrung!" he answered fiercely, at the same time putting his arms around her and holding her close. Karenza gave a little sigh of contentment as she rested her head against his shoulder.